AFTER?

An alumnus of St Stephen's College in the University of Delhi, **Nidhi Dalmia** pursued post graduate education at Oxford University and the Sorbonne and post experience Management education at Harvard Business School. His professional life exposed him to managing various factories.

Nidhi cherishes the spiritual environment prevalent in his home, where Vedas, Upanishads were a part of his home schooling.

Nidhi's father, Ramkrishna Dalmia was one of the top three industrialists in India, who rose as a self-made entrepreneur, in a career spanning both British India and free India. His visit to the UK and the US in the early 1950s in pursuit of his ideal of One World Government got considerable media attention in the US.

This is Nidhi's second novel. His first novel Harp was released in 2016 and received critical acclaim from leading newspapers and magazines including the *Hindustan Times*, *Deccan Chronicle*, among others.

Nidhi was in his college table tennis team at Oxford and also enjoys Tennis and Swimming. His interests include Cinema, Theatre, Western Pop, Folk and Classical music. At heart Nidhi is a wanderer and a romantic.

He divides his time between Delhi and Paris.

Reach him at:

http://www.twitter.com/nidhidalmiaharp

http://www.facebook.com/nidhidalmiaharp

http://www.instagram.com/nidhidalmiaharp

https://in.linkedin.com/in/gun-nidhi-dalmia-3458135.

http://www.gunnidhidalmia.com

'Nidhi Dalmia's imaginative writing set in Delhi, Kashmir and Berkeley, USA evokes nostalgia for another era, offering a poetic glimpse into the intensity of love and longing in the swinging sixties.'

—**Siddharth Kak**, Popular Television Personality and Author

'Refreshing, vivid account of the protagonist growing up in New Delhi in the swinging '60s and travelling to the US, exploring human relations unselfconsciously. Great nostalgia for the '60s generations of young Indians and Americans.'

—**Salman Khurshid**, Author and former Indian Minister of External Affairs

'War, love, travel. The sixties India. In his seductive tale of love and longing, Nidhi Dalmia takes us into a world of free spirits constrained by familiar doubts. A delightful read.'

—**Sanjaya Baru**, Economist, Writer and Media Personality

'Set in the Bay Area, New York, Kashmir, and Delhi in the late 1960s, intertwined with the significant cultural, student, sexual, and intellectual revolutions taking place then, *Afternoon* is a moving tale that superlatively reflects how our lives are shaped by the choices we make as well as factors beyond our control.

—**Sandeep Bamzai**, Veteran Journalist and Author

'A riveting narration of one man's journey across borders, spanning a conflicted landscape of love, loss, and courage to discover meaning in the parables of history.'

—**Ravi Shankar Etteth**, Author of *The Tiger by the River*, *The Brahmin*, and *Killing Time in Delhi*

'In today's age of social media and instant gratification, *Afternoon* is a pleasant reminder of how humanity thrives on culture, cross-border relationships, and empathy.'

—**Raghavendra Rathore**, Design Mentor

'*Afternoon* is a fascinating story bringing alive the mood, atmosphere and the hidden undercurrents of societies of the '60s. The term afternoon representing the waning of day and slowing of rhythms, is aptly reflected in the book through challenges faced in inter-relationships set amid international geo-politics, choices made and acceptance of factors beyond anyone's control, all of which have been subtly interwoven by the author, Nidhi Dalmia.'

—**Shovana Narayan**, Kathak Guru, IAAS retd., and Author

Praise for the author's debut novel, *Harp*

'*Harp* by Nidhi Dalmia is a refreshing love story. [It] explores what happens when two people from completely different universes meet. A unique, touching love story set in the times of communist Poland of the late sixties—the Iron Curtain forms the backdrop of the story… Dalmia's book offers a mix of characters and takes the reader through their remarkable journey, making this a must read. It is well written, racy and colourful…'

—*Hindustan Times*

'A deftly crafted and consistently compelling read from beginning to end, *Harp* is an extraordinarily entertaining novel that clearly documents author Nidhi Dalmia as an original, skilled and innately talented storyteller.'

—*Midwest Book Review*, Oregon, Washington

'The book deals with journeys we make across countries, even as we embark on a private quest within to know ourselves better, and to seek what it is we really want from life.'

—*Business Standard*

'Nidhi Dalmia… Sculpts *Harp*, a fiction about love, longing and coming of age… Encompassing these journeys is also a quest on their part to know themselves better and seek what they really want. These aspects' reflecting real life situations and the universality of emotions resonates well with the reader.'

—The Hindu

'*Harp* is a moving book that talks about love, sacrifice and passion. It is a romantic fiction that transports one to the late sixties and all the changes taking place then… *Harp* also gives a description of socio-economic situation in India and abroad prevalent at the time. It has elements of the Dairy Industry and Business management.'

—India Today Education

'Love, longing and coming of age intertwined with cultural, sexual, student revolutions and the music of the '60s.'

—Deccan Chronicle

'With degrees from Oxford and Harvard under his belt, he took a decades-long detour to the world of business before finally telling a story close to his heart.'

—The Tribune

'Nidhi Dalmia's debut novel, *Harp*, resonates the words of Charles Dickens as he paints the picture of a dreamy romantic world and transports his readers to 1960s. It's a tale of three friends, Ashok, Lauren and Aparna, told through twists and turns, many emotional voyages traversing through the Europe less travelled.'

—The New Indian Express

AFTERNOON

NIDHI DALMIA

RUPA

Published by
Rupa Publications India Pvt. Ltd 2023
7/16, Ansari Road, Daryaganj
New Delhi 110002

Sales centres:
Prayagraj Bengaluru Chennai
Hyderabad Jaipur Kathmandu
Calcutta Mumbai

P-ISBN: 978-93-5702-111-1
E-ISBN: 978-93-5702-114-2

First impression 2023

10 9 8 7 6 5 4 3 2 1

To Amba

Joe

1

'Noooo! You didn't! I wasn't aware of anyone noticing anything. Least of all you.'

She gave a knowing smile and then an enigmatic one. She pulled up the elastic band of Rajiv's underwear and peeked in. 'Gosh! That's really blooming,' she said.

'Hey, who asked you to peek?' he said, taken aback.

'C'mon! I'm many years older than you,' she said, pulling down his underwear. Joe had been his class teacher since the previous year.

The school had decided to have the same teacher in the last two years of school, since these were such critical years and results of the School Leaving Exams were so important in shaping each pupil's future, especially in those days, not to mention the school's own image. For the very same reason, Rajiv's parents had decided to hire her for private tuition as well some months before the Board exams.

Rajiv's was a boys' school and there wasn't much exposure to girls, except for the occasional Social with a neighbouring Convent. However, there were friends of friends in nearby Man Nagar who went to co-ed schools and through whom Rajiv had started going to dance parties in the last year of school. Fox Trot, Samba, Tango, Waltz, Twisting and Jiving were the order of the day and both the boys and the girls were quite skilled.

The light grew more intense as the sun went over the horizon. Unconstrained, it really swayed gigantically like a mad elephant.

'See what I mean?' she laughed again. He felt a soft hand

on his hot, burning erection. It became even stiffer with her touch. As it bloomed and swayed like an oak tree, Joe stared at it in fascination.

'I didn't know it could get as huge as this,' she laughed again. 'I saw it bulging inside your underwear.'

'Did you never see it like that?'

'Well, once. Some afternoons ago. My God! What were you thinking just before the lesson? How come it was big then?'

Rajiv smiled mysteriously, actually not remembering the incident at all.

'I wasn't thinking anything sexy. These things just happen sometimes, come sometimes. No reason.'

'Strange, you guys are.'

'What's so strange about it? Sometimes there just are erections. Who knows why? Haven't you heard of morning erections? Maybe it needs to get bigger to hold back the susu which builds up, as another control mechanism.'

'Morning erections is one thing …'

She bent down and peered at it curiously some more. She ran her hand up and down, getting a feel of it. She examined it from various angles. She moved her hand under his testicles. Such strange and curious things these are, her expression unmistakably said. Her hand felt so cool.

'Joe?'

'What?'

'Nothing.'

She went on with her Geography lesson. The latitude of the temperate zone in Siberia, its produce, how it differed from the temperate zone in the West. There were a lot of facts to absorb and remember. The lesson ended before the light totally faded.

'What are you doing being big again, pray?'

'It's automatic. Am not even aware of it.'

The song 'Teacher's Pet', which would be broadcast often on All India Radio's *A Date With You* on Friday nights, played in his head. There was a kiss on the inside cover, of Rock Hudson kissing a very pretty star. Her chin completely rested on his. They were fully into it. 'Why is she enjoying it so much?' he thought. 'Do girls also like it? Openly?' It really turned him on. Just like the kiss on the cover of *From Here to Eternity*—lying on the beach, kissing at an angle, mouth fully covering the other's, skin against skin.

In another one, the sky was dark in a friendly, enveloping sort of way; maybe it was dawn or dusk. No one was around. A couple were sitting in the middle of the beach, on their knees on the yellowish sand. They had wet, clinging swimming clothes. Their lean, taut bodies, which seemed dark and attractive in that light, were tightly clasped. They were kissing passionately. It was as if the camera was zooming in on the panorama from far away. It was a black and white photograph and heightened the portrayal.

Of such imagery were born fantasies and sleepless nights, before Joe had come into Rajiv's sheltered life.

He had wanted to try everything, he told Joe. He had read about loggers. Mighty men. He was still not strong. His arms were thin. But he wanted to try it. There was a thin tree, maybe as young as himself or maybe only slightly older. He decided to try it, one day. He found an axe in the tool shed and started cutting it. He had to keep axing at the same place to make an impression. Gradually, it began to form and the green of the young tree began to show. Why was he doing it? He wanted to experience it. Was he hurting the tree? Was the tree crying out? It was only a tree. Wasn't an animal. He looked around. None of the malis came. They were lost in the haze of the afternoon. Yet, something was happening. He kept doing it. He had to succeed. He hadn't picked a giant tree with a big, thick trunk. He was killing an innocent tree. It had done nothing. He kept feeling uneasy at the same time. 'But why?' he thought. He wasn't doing anything wrong. He was accomplishing something. Adding that experience. Proving to himself that he could do it. No family member interrupted him. It was taking longer than he had expected. The dent in the tree kept getting deeper. He had done it. The tree fell. The large mango tree next to it, with its many branches, was a silent witness to what had happened to the little tree.

He described some of his childhood to her.

'When I was a little boy, at times I wanted to be a girl. Sometimes I longed for it. I must have been seven or eight then. I was ashamed of these thoughts. I hid them from everyone but not from myself. Boys seemed so rough and tough, so competitive. I didn't want to jump into that fray. Girls were so soft and gentle, dainty and gracious, sensitive, and altogether desirable. I liked their pastel-coloured frocks, the way they laughed and giggled and flirted even then. I wanted to hold them, be held by them.

'On the other hand, I didn't at all want to be a girl. Imagine being attracted to boys! Imagine kissing them! Yuck! I didn't want to be a girlish boy either. I'd be considered a sissy. And girls may not be attracted to me. They might want a manly type. If I liked them so much, for that reason alone I had to develop my masculine qualities. But they were so needlessly aggressive. I had to be that? So insensitive sometimes. That's why I liked women.

'Professor Higgins was right—in his own context, I agreed with him when I saw the movie. But he got it wrong as well—isn't that the nature of everything—why couldn't boys be more like girls? Attributes like empathy, gracefulness, flexibility; qualities like softness, gentleness, kindness. Degrees did matter. How can you be so fond of a whole sex? Attracted to a whole gender? Was there something wrong with me?

'In our main hall, on a set of sofas sat a group of ladies, as I wandered by innocently. I must have been no more than three then. One of them, in the corner nearest me, pouted her lips and beckoned to me. She was very fair, with sharp features. She must have been in her 20s but seemed so grown up to me then. I hesitated but didn't show it. Did she sense it? She pouted her lips in an even more pronounced fashion. It was clear that she was inviting me to come and get a kiss on the lips. There was something very attractive about her. She was wearing a red sleeveless blouse which showed off her glistening rounded shoulders and smooth, fair arms. She invited me again, her lips protruding together. I wanted very much to be kissed by her.

'But I didn't dare. I couldn't really do that. Maybe it was my upbringing. I looked at her, certain that I wasn't revealing anything. Then drifted away.'

His mother's spacious cupboard seemed so full of treasures. He and the other children liked to rummage around when she opened it but she wouldn't let them. And the back of the almirah, in fact, slid open, revealing a secret room, where she kept her jewellery and a pistol for their protection. She did not want to even acknowledge its presence as she feared accidents. There were other places in the house, with hollow sounds. The children went around a la Enid Blyton mysteries, tapping at walls and ornate teakwood mantelpieces and fireplaces, expecting to stumble upon a secret passage, places containing ancient secrets and who knows, even precious jewels and other treasures from the time of the previous inhabitants.

Rajiv showed Joe a large ancient tub in the bathroom. It had a transparent glass panel on three sides, forming a guard box around the shower. It gave him a nice enclosed feeling. It had elaborate sprinklers at the sides, which made fancy things happen inside the panel. The taps would fill the tub below, the shower would be on at the same time. When he was very little, he could stand there for hours. His parents thought of Shiva, standing there motionless on Kailash, with the Ganga flowing down on his head from above and cascading to the earth.

He and his siblings, joined sometimes by assorted cousins, played innumerable imaginative games, many of them self-created. Some of the slightly older ones acted out plays in Hindi, while the others watched—plays taken from the Mahabharat, the 18 Puranas, stories of Vikramaditya, Akbar-Birbal, Padmini, tales of treachery, intrigue, of princes going hunting—galloping on imaginary horses all across the drawing room. One of the plays involved a teacher in the middle and a student on either side. The teacher, in Bhugol, would say, 'Repeat after me: *Prithvi gol hai.*' The students' responses were so funny that the younger children would fall off the sofa laughing.

The drawing room was a lovely dark place, full of cool colours during the extremely hot summer. It had several darkish blue sofas. There was a gap behind the sofas, along which the children crawled while playing Dark Room. The sofas had cushions with black brocade and silk covers with lovely designs on them, blue curtains on door rods across the French windows. The Den would go outside and count. The room was made pitch black. There were small stools, *modas*, tables, numerous bits of furniture in the spacious room, which added to the unexpected. As the Den made her or his way, he could bump into anything, scrape his knee against a table or trip over something, make something fall.

It was also supposed to be one of the haunted rooms in this house, which gave many a visitor the shivers just going up the middle staircase and down the dark gallery upstairs, even in the afternoon, when it would be very bright outside. Some of the salon like rooms had these special feelings about them, as did their verandahs.

It was part of the folklore of the house. Some of the servants spoke of a limping shadow that was often seen at night near the gate. Safety lay in numbers, as there were so many playing. It was also allowed to make sounds; the boys usually chose scary ones to scare the girls. Rajiv crawled along behind the sofas; maybe he'd bump into someone.

On summer evenings the children's beds would be spread on the cool green lawns, under a canopy of mosquito nets; the horse riding and tales from ancient books would extend to the vastness of the lawns.

Joe was charmed.

Some classes later, the lesson was not to start for another 15 minutes. Rajiv was standing. Joe came into the room. The huge bulge under his trousers caught the eye. He would have turned his thoughts to produce of the Tundra region but she had caught him unprepared.

'Is that thing always bursting from your trousers?'

Rajiv blushed. 'I have to finish early today, so I came earlier. I had no way of telling you.'

It was a classic blue covered Geography text book. They turned to pictures of Russian boys and girls sewing sheepskin coats. He thought of Siberia. The lesson was interesting but there were too many facts to absorb. He had done map work also. She held his hand and showed him how to do it better. He got an electric shock. She must have got it too. She glanced down and laughed. This time it was buttons. It was hard to undo them. Once released from that restraint, the elastic of the underwear was once again summarily dealt with. Her hand cool and white against the redness of the object with a mind of its own, lingered longer this time in the area.

Rajiv decided to confide in his teacher. Something unique had happened to him sometime back. One day he was lying on the big bed with his face down. He was thinking of the many mags under the mattress, not to mention the comics of all description and picture library books from England, as they were called. The long school day was over. He changed out of his uniform and lay thankfully on the bed. He started very slowly moving up and down. It was very satisfying. He felt the pressure down below but wasn't specifically conscious of it. The whole afternoon must have passed or so it seemed. His thoughts were on girls and the thrills that lay in store in his unfolding life.

The slow languorous movement and corresponding enjoyment increased, built up very gradually. It seemed to be getting ever more pleasurable. Suddenly, he had an unbelievable sensation. There were really no words for it. Everything seemed to explode into fireworks. There were stars everywhere. What had happened? He had no idea. Could it happen again? He had discovered something unknown. It was a Discovery. But why in this realm? Why couldn't it have been something scientific, for example? Something great. Instead of a shameful secret that was no use to mankind. It would help no one. 'This will just make us unfit for sports, turn us into weaklings and sissys, unable to compete in the tough meat-eating world of men,' he brooded. It had been very enjoyable but he should forget all about it. Not indulge in it again.

Some days later he lay down again and it happened again. And again after a few days. There was a feeling of exultation, Whoosh, it would go and there would be fountains. There would be lovely music and he'd be dancing like a dervish, until, of course, the guilt set in.

Rajiv would drink an extra glass of milk to recover his waning strength. Sometimes he'd join a group of friends for tennis. There'd be several friends. Gautam, older than him, would look at his sunken cheeks, on days that he'd done it twice or even thrice, give him a piercing look and say, '*Aarey, aaj to bahut kar liya*'. 'Could he possibly know?' Rajiv thought. Since it was his discovery. But he seemed to know something. He only said it on those days of excess. What was he talking about?

Rajiv tried several times to stop. But he would lie down and it would happen again. In the meantime, he'd discovered a different method. He didn't have to lie on his stomach and put pressure on parts below. He could do it much faster but still long enough to enjoy it with his hands. And he was much more in control. Sometimes he succeeded in stopping for as long as a month. But then he would fall prey to temptation again and he would feel that that whole effort had been wasted.

Joe's smile spread to the corner of her eyes—she told him that it was quite common, he needn't feel guilty, that it was another form of sexuality and that it was quite OK. She said it with confidence. She seemed to know. It was very reassuring. Joe put him much more at ease with sexuality. He would always be grateful.

Joe's elder brother had joined the Air Force. The Services in India have a lot of perks, are respected and generally well liked by most professions in India, otherwise caste ridden, including the Business-Government divide.

In India's caste conscious society, modern professions had taken the place of the old castes. The new Caste was superimposed on the old ones and to a certain extent, replaced. But Caste consciousness was very deeply ingrained, including amongst the educated. If a Kshatriya became a Wing Commander he was doubly respected for being both but more for being a Wing Commander.

Perquisites, facilities, cheap and, to an extent, free booze in the Mess and many other things subsidised did not make up for very low salaries. So, there were a lot of other things but hardly any cash to spend on nice things to be purchased, holidays, savings for children's education abroad.

Officers and men in the Army, Navy and Air Force continued to retire at ages once considered old, though many of them were in the prime of their lives at the time of retirement, with the country having invested a lot in their training and attaining excellence. Substantial increase in longevity over the decades was not sufficiently taken into account and people from the Services retired too early.

Her brother had been hired to run a flying club and she to teach in a school. The salaries were much higher in Australia. He was far from retirement but had served enough years to be able to voluntarily relinquish service, should a better opportunity arise.

They became yet another Anglo-Indian family migrating to Australia in the '50s and '60s. Her father, a prominent broadcaster on All India Radio, as well as a much-loved cricket commentator, had also got an offer from Radio Australia.

Most Anglo-Indians migrated above all to Australia, followed by the UK, with New Zealand, Canada, and the US a distant third. They migrated for a better standard of living and a cultural milieu they thought they would be more at home with. However, acceptance from all accounts by local populations was not as anticipated, nor what had been hoped for. From 1 million at the time of Independence, the Anglo-Indian population dwindled to about 150,000 and thereafter even less.

In its earlier days, the East India Company was in favour of their soldiers marrying local women because of the difficulty of getting sufficient English women to India. It was reported that they even gave such couples a few silver rupees for each

Anglo-Indian child born. The Madras Presidency was one of the first to move in this direction. Even the official definition for a long time was not that of one parent English and the other Indian but the father English and the mother Indian.

Many state legislatures and the Indian Parliament had two seats reserved for Anglo-Indians right up to January 2020. They were prominent Anglo-Indians nominated by the government to represent their community, Frank Anthony, President of the All India Anglo-Indian Association, being the most prominent of them.

Anglo-Indians were prominent in education, broadcasting and sports. Some of them became administrators in British Companies headquartered in Calcutta. They also went for the tea estates in Assam and Darjeeling, settling down to the very colonial lifestyle over there, of vast and beautiful vistas, earlier mornings than farther west in India, then 'tennis anyone' and tea in the evening. But many of them also had issues of not belonging. Some, who'd never been to England, still spoke of it as 'back Home' and found their culture different from mainstream Indian. Others found that they weren't fully accepted back Home. Some, like Vivien Leigh, Engelbert Humperdinck, made it big. Some like Merle Oberon chose to obfuscate the Anglo-Indian part of it.

There was also confusion about a group of English who had been born in India and had spent all or most of their lives in India. They too were called Anglo-Indians. They couldn't quite settle down to life in England when they tried to live there after a lifetime with the sights and smells of India.

Rajiv's school Final exams got over in December 1964. The family had been planning to leave around then. The arrangements, the migration, employment and housing papers of Joe's family took a long time. Inevitably, much longer than expected. When the different pieces fell in place and everything came together, it happened suddenly. The family finally managed to leave in February 1966. They left with eight and a half dollars per person in their pockets. That was all that was allowed by the Government of India.

When the last day of Class was over, Joe told her Class she would stay in touch. Rajiv's tuition continued during the Exams. On the last day of tuition, Joe gave him a present. She smiled dazzlingly and kissed him. 'You are a sweet boy; you will go far. I will miss you,' she said.

In the time that followed, Rajiv thought about her; she had been a very good teacher. She had had a formative influence but nobody in Class heard from her again.

Ayesha

1

Six months passed between school and college as per the system those days. The School Leaving Exam would be in December and college would start only in July. Indian parents, ever conscious of their children's education, made sure that the children didn't have a long holiday, while the children, recovering from the rigours of school in general and the all-important School Leaving Exam, tried their best to have precisely that.

The parties had started even before college. There were friends of friends in similar schools which were co-ed, as well as nearby colonies and Army, Navy, Air Force Officers' messes.

China had attacked India suddenly in October 1962 through some of the world's coldest and most inaccessible terrain in Leach. Rajiv was still in school and struggling with the burdens of 9th class. Physics and Chemistry had already become quite onerous but unlike 10th class, when they had to choose between Science and other streams, Geography and its maps were quite advanced and the workload was heavy. 9th class was notorious for being one of the toughest years.

India was taken completely by surprise, though it should not have been, as the Chinese, not satisfied with their occupation of Tibet, had gradually, little by little, quietly been eating into Indian territory in eastern Leach on the plateau of Aksai Chin, unchallenged by India. There were some coughs from India when they announced that they had built a road but the Indian Government chose to look the other way. Nehru, when questioned, said in his infamous justification 'not a blade of grass grows in' that area. No one asked him if it was so worthless why China wanted it and why it was spending resources in building infrastructure and deploying its Army over there. More territory gives strategic advantage and future technology may have uses for materials and minerals underneath. In the war, India suffered a humiliating defeat. Some of the Indian elite thought themselves successors of the Imperial British but they were not. China captured an area of Ladakh almost the size of Switzerland. Up till now, there had been talk of Hindi-Chini bhai. But China had been smouldering about India giving shelter to the Dalai Lama and other Tibetan refugees. Mao and Chou En Lai took a decision to teach India a lesson. The People's Liberation Army had defeated the Nationalists in the whole of China. Their numbers were high and they were well equipped for fighting in the snow and ice. The Indian media described them as coming like gajar-mooli. More and more just kept pouring down the passes.

Gen Ayub thought he could do the same in Kashmir. Surprise and strategy. The Indian Army was outnumbered in certain sectors when the attack started. He would come away the winner.

The 1965 Indo-Pak War had begun with rumours about infiltrators coming into Kashmir from across the border. These became small daily news items in the Press until the scale of it became such that it led to a full-scale war. Rajiv and Ayesha had the unusual experience of blackouts at night and the sound of wailing sirens whenever there was the imminent threat of Delhi being bombed. It wasn't so far from the border. College parties continued during the black outs, the dark giving them drama and adventure. The potential of subterranean sensuality. European diplomats whose parents had experienced the Second World War scoffed. 'This isn't war,' they said, with pregnant emphasis on 'War'. The 8 a.m. siren became a daily ritual just to make sure it was in good working order. It continues to this day, except at some stage and for some reason, 8 a.m. became 9 a.m.

The war lasted from April to September. Things didn't turn out for Gen Ayub as per plan. Pakistani infiltration came to a halt and the objective of launching a full-scale insurgency in Kashmir was not achieved, despite the use of Patton tanks by Pakistan, given to it by its CENTO ally, the US, to fight against Communism.

Indian Prime Minister Lal Bahadur Shastri signed a peace accord in Tashkent, facilitated by the Soviet Union, with the tall and cherubic Pathan military dictator Field Marshal Ayub Khan.

The next morning, Shastri unexpectedly passed away. There were subdued rumours of foul play in Delhi later but nothing came of those. Great Power Games had been on since Yalta.

In Delhi the party scene got back on its feet, with Francoise Hardy's 'Tous les garcons et les filles' and other beautiful songs: 'Satisfaction'[1], 'Downtown' by Petula Clark, 'My Girl' by The Temptations, 'Silhouettes' by Herman's Hermits, 'I'll Never Find Another You' by The Seekers, 'Ticket to Ride'[2]to name but a few.

The Twist was still in its heyday as was the ever eye-catching Jive, the Cha Cha interspersed with the Fox Trot. There were a number of boys and girls who could Waltz very well. Many of them had parents in the Armed Forces. The Shake was beginning to disturb the pre-eminence of the Twist.

'Walk Don't Run '64' had hit the charts, now 65 was speeding along.

Drain pipes were the order of the day for boys, with pointed shoes and buckles and sometimes clips in the soles of their feet to tap to Elvis movies. Or there were inviting movie halls to watch movies like *The Sound of Music, Help, A Patch of Blue* and *Those Magnificent Men in Their Flying Machines.*

Girls wore tight salwar kameez or gorgeous saris.

Herzog and *Up the Down Staircase* came out to be read, as did *Armageddon.*

Wajahat was one of the three MPs from Kashmir, belonging to the ruling party in the State legislature. He had been allotted one of the flats meant for MPs right next to King Edward Road Officers Mess. His daughter Ayesha soon became very good friends with Rajiv's sister in the neighbourhood.

As both entered the First Year in Delhi University, in their respective girls and boys only colleges, close by, within the Campus, their interests grew as their horizons expanded. Ayesha remained Rajiv's sister's close friend, until that first unexpected encounter with Rajiv the spring of the next year.

In College, it suddenly went to the other extreme from the British Public School atmosphere of his school. Rajiv enjoyed the new found freedom. There were even more parties to go to—in Defence Colony, in Greater Kailash, in Jor Bagh, Malcha Marg and Vasant Vihar and other neighbourhoods in Delhi- Colonies as they were called. His college was not co-ed, nor was Ayesha's, but they were both colleges infused with the liberal, intellectual ethos of the time. There was plenty of exposure to the other sex not just at parties but at many university-level happenings, film clubs, Sitar and other classical music concerts and above all, auditions for plays put up in Rajiv's college, Ayesha's and several other colleges in and outside the Campus, but part of Delhi University. They went to the auditorium on Ring Road, where they watched avant-garde movies screened by the difficult to get into university film society, Celluloid. There were also several other groups like Yatrik and Youth of India. The plays necessarily had to have boys and girls and a lot of play practice was involved in the college where it was being put up. Dates followed these events to movies, poetry readings or just for a coffee at the Indian Coffee House, situated between both their colleges. There was also the college café with its pseudo-intellectual atmosphere, with each person trying to outdo the other in their manifest sophistication.

Wajahat's urban outpost was in Srinagar, where they had a handicrafts business. Ayesha's grandfather had found himself on the other side of Kashmir, at the time of the unexpected and sudden partition of the sub-continent and even more unexpected partition of Kashmir a bit later.

Since centuries, Kashmir's culture had evolved to be composite despite the mass conversion in the 14th century. In the syncretic culture, the meat eating Kashmiri Pandits and the Muslim majority lived entirely at ease with each other without the consciousness of who is what. Amongst those that were converted, Dhars became Dars, for example, and Bhatts became Butts.

The flat had, amongst other things, pictures of vast saffron fields, apple orchards and walnut trees from the Kashmiri landscape near Srinagar, as well as their farm, which just the other day had been a reality.

Their large ancestral land was in the portion of Kashmir which had been run over by the invading Pathan irregulars with loyalties to none but nominally on behalf of the newly formed state of Pakistan, whose own army was coming into being from Muslim officers of the British Indian Army.[3]

Whenever Parliament was in recess and when there were summer holidays for schools and colleges, the family went to Kashmir every chance they got. Srinagar was just an hour's flight away and as an MP, Wajahat was entitled to free passages for him and his family between Parliament and his constituency. Kashmir was the only State where the Monsoon didn't come, so it was open season even during the months of July and August. Sometimes, Wajahat went alone to tend to his constituency and just to enjoy home.

In mid-August 1947, when India and Pakistan became free, the Maharaja could not immediately decide about what his princely state should do—be independent, join India or Pakistan. Both he and Sheikh Abdullah, the local politician who had become prominent, were inclined towards India for different reasons. Sheikh Abdullah wanted to have a secular, democratic Kashmir.

'In late October, with the connivance of sections of Pakistan's armed forces, a large force of tribesmen from the North West Frontier entered the princely state and quickly overwhelmed Maharaja Hari Singh's army.' The Maharaja fled to his Palace in Jammu and signed the instrument of accession to India. [4]

Sheikh Abdullah manoeuvred into 'the vacuum created by the flight of the Maharaja with Communist help' and his supporters flooded the streets. The main heart looked like Red Square with the National Conference red flag everywhere. [5]

The Indian Army stopped the takeover of Kashmir but failed to evict the tribesmen from the western part of Kashmir and the northern areas and the State abruptly became partitioned.

Margaret Bourke-White, the famous *Life* photographer, was one of the few international journalists who was resourceful and determined enough to be witness to this from both sides. Access was considered impossible but she somehow managed to get to Abbottabad from the Pakistani side to talk to the Pathan invaders.

She wrote, 'Sometimes their help to their brother Muslims in Kashmir was accomplished so quickly that they came back within a day or two only to return to Kashmir with more tribesmen, to repeat their indiscriminate "liberating" and terrorising of Hindu,

Muslim, Sikh villagers alike.' They returned after each foray, bursting with loot.

She saw a desecrated Convent in Baramulla, the Mission Hospital ransacked. The Kashmir Valley bore the wounds of the Tribesmen's invasions for a long time.

'Should the invaders come again a self-defence force of Kashmiris was launched. This civil militia included women, to help defend Srinagar and particularly to protect the honour of women. The women were provided with rifles and trained in their use. Hindus, Muslims, Sikhs fought together to keep the raiders out. There was an exemplary display of Kashmiri unity. There were persistent reports of extensive sexual violence by the invaders in Baramulla and a number of young Sikh women were abducted. The men's self-defence militia saw active service alongside Indian troops.' [6]

Sayed Haider Raza portrayed some of this in his watercolour 'Baramulla in Ruins', 1948.

Wajahat's sister and Ayesha's bua, Aamna, lived on the farms along with their parents. They got letters from them except when there was fighting between India and Pakistan. It was a cosmopolitan Kashmiri upper-class family and both sides of the family reflected those values.

Both sides dreamt of the days when lasting peace would be arrived at so that they could freely visit the other side again. It didn't seem so far off then. The family suddenly got separated— on either side, with the Maharaja's army overwhelmed and the Pathans irregulars over running Kashmir very swiftly and unexpectedly. There was so much chaos, upheaval and terror that Wajahat and his family could not go to the area under the ransacking fighters, nor vice versa. But they thought that things would settle down and then they would go.

Owing to what they suffered at the hands of Pathan invaders

at the time of Freedom—even local Muslims fought them off. It wasn't seen as Muslim-Hindu then. The attackers had the advantage of having done so immediately. There had been no time to anticipate, leave alone prepare. They would go back with their pillage, turn around and be back within two-three days for more, their primary gain being the loot and the women.

Internal Pakistani politics had an immediate and direct impact on Kashmir. The amicable spirit of the Nehru-Liaquat pact, including about abducted women, their rights, forced conversions, etc. would only get better, it was hoped. For a while there was this atmosphere.

Muslim families in India who had stayed behind could change their minds and move to Pakistan, attracted by hopes of a more affluent life. But a number of things happened for different complex reasons, not the least of them being Great Power rivalry to vitiate this.

Things moved fast on the political front in Pakistan [7] Liaqat Ali himself was assassinated soon after in October 1951. In 1956 it became an Islamic Republic, ending its status as a Dominion of the British Empire. There was a new Constitution. Two years saw four Prime Ministers. Ayub Khan, the Army Chief, used this instability to seize power and declared martial law in 1958. The coup was also supported by the United States, a flag bearer of democracy.

The Army's importance coming from a state of war with India, there were several military dictators who ruled Pakistan for many years. Army rule was interspersed with periods of democratically elected Prime Ministers but even at those times, the Army remained powerful.

The political culture of Pakistan with its three As became well-known—Army, Allah and America.

Tension with India became more or less a given, belying

Jinnah's original thought of two friendly neighbours with free and easy movement between the two.

As late as 1937, Hayat Khan was elected Premier of Punjab province in Lahore. His government was opposed to the idea of Pakistan. His untimely tragic death and civil disobedience by the Muslim League caused the fall of his Unionist Ministry.

Khan Abdul Ghaffar Khan—the Frontier Gandhi—too had opposed the idea of Pakistan. He was the dominant political figure in the North West Frontier Province. Despite his stature, he was imprisoned from September 1948 to January 1954, even though he was a member of the Constituent Assembly.

Once the creation of a separate state in a very short period of time was achieved, the *raison d'etre* of the Muslim League disappeared. Jinnah himself passed away within a year. There was conflict over how to implement Islam. Governor Generals Ghulam Muhammad and Iskander Mirza (later President) far from being titular heads, dismissed four Prime Ministers—Nazimuddin, Suhrawardy, Chundrigar and Feroz Khan Noon. Iskander Mirza imposed martial law but three weeks later was himself deposed by his own Army Chief Ayub Khan, sent into exile in London, never to return, forced, as per some rumours, into a waiting car in the middle of the night, clad in his night clothes, with little resistance from his guards. [8]

Not all Indian-Muslims had supported the Muslim League; many of their prominent intellectuals had found the idea ludicrous, but their rapid rise in just a few years after conception of the Pakistan idea as late as the mid-1930s by a group of Indian-Muslim students at Cambridge, Rehamat Ali prominent among them, was due to the Congress' active role in the Quit India movement and the war time jailing of their leaders. They lost a lot of ground, particularly amongst the Muslims in that period and the British, sensing an opportunity to divide and rule, particularly with Churchill (virulently opposed to Independence for India, to losing the Jewel in the Crown of the Empire) at the helm, patronised the Muslim League, helping in their meteoric rise in a very short span of time. Insecurities were fanned and played upon and they had an open field with no one to challenge them. The Muslim League, a party supported by landlords as late as 1937, quickly came around to the idea of a separate State.

The Pakistan idea, dismissed at the time as fanciful and students' dreams, as quickly as 1940 became the Lahore Declaration adopted by the Muslim League. Rehamat Ali himself was expelled in 1948 from Pakistan by Liaqat Ali Khan and died a pauper in Cambridge in 1951, with even his funeral expenses being borne by the Master of his College in Cambridge.

2

Ayesha described exceedingly beautiful spots in Kashmir to Rajiv's sister and whoever of the family happened to be around in the Afternoon at tea time. Wondrous places redolent of clouds, vistas with which every monarch fell in love.

There were spellbinding panoramas, saffron fields, other vales that made up the rice bowl of Kashmir for the staple Kashmiri diet of lamb and rice. Sometimes, they would go over to her house near King Edward Road mess and Wajahat would show slides. It was magic; these places would come alive.

They showed Baramulla (earlier named Varah Mul), with its temple, its lake and its history.

There was Yusmarg, one of the many gems with which Kashmir is studded and the nearby NilNag (blue serpent) Lake.

The kitchen in Ayesha's house in Kashmir was to the side, in a separate small room connected by a dark and windy corridor with latticed walls on either side. But it had a cheerful, crackling fire in it on which hot rotis, swelling with warm air inside, were prepared and served along with steaming hot vegetables. The family ate quickly, eager to escape the dark and cold night outside. As May would progress to June, the nights would become milder and moonlit. The sun was bright and beautiful in the tall chinar trees outside. The drawing room had large windows. The panorama *dehors* seemed to be from an impressionist painting.

They talked about Srinagar, of course, with its ineffable charm, Nishat and Shalimar Gardens, Dal and Nagin lakes with their beautiful and comfortable houseboats and water skiing, the tiny, romantic Char Chinar island right in the middle of Dal Lake, to go where in a boat with a loved one was to go somewhere else; Chasma Shahi in Srinagar, constructed by Shah Jahan, the Shankaracharya temple on top of the mountain, its residential colonies like Raj Bagh with their cherry trees inside residential gardens, the spacious Convent next door, the boulevards with the trees hiding the bungalows on either side, Jhelum River with its shikara crossings, and the lakes dotted with shikaras ferrying fruits, vegetables, goods for sale or tourists. Walnut trees even on the way in from the Airport, its bustling older parts of the city to name just some of its attractions. Srinagar's mystique exemplified that of the rest of Kashmir. There were bridges into the older parts of town, a path leading to Nehru Park with its Café, the resplendent Palace Hotel at a height overlooking Srinagar, with large rooms opening on to a spacious lawn. Shikara wallahs haggled with tourists to ferry them across the Jhelum. Even children were not spared.

Ayesha recounted one of the first times she had gotten on to a water ski in Nageen Lake. There were two house boats from which the motor boats took off. They were full of foreigners for some reason. She was scared. Her older cousin said he would be on the water ski with her and coaxed her to get on. As the jet boat took off, to her horror she saw that her cousin had tricked her and was not standing behind her on the water skis. The sudden start of the boat made her fall on the water surface and the speed of the boat, as she held on, pulled her horizontally. She did a whole round of the lake like that. She felt a lot of eyes on her. By the time the next round started she had managed to pick herself up while still being pulled and to stand. The next round she did *comme il faut* and she felt a sense of exhilaration.

There were book shops across the Jhelum with lovely smelling books, orange-coloured Penguins, multi coloured Pans, Dells, hard backs with PG Wodehouse, Arthur Conan Doyle, Somerset Maugham, Nevil Shute and Agatha Christie, where you could spend a rainy afternoon and then again step out into a spectacular evening, with the street lights being reflected in the puddles outside. Some couples held hands. It was the ultimate romantic place.

The restaurants and bars had atmosphere, were full of life, with couples doing the Cha Cha in perfect harmony to the latest music. Attractive couples caught the eye as they executed the Jive perfectly with exactly balancing tension, the light-coloured dupatta of the girls' air-borne with the movement, when they were in salwar kameezzes, to music that made you want to get up and dance at Premier and Capri. Premier played with softly spotlighting the dance floor, so it seemed like out of the movies. It would be difficult to be blue over there.

The movie halls showed *Come September* and *Charade*. Wills Cigarette Co ran a campaign—'Made for each other'.

Then it would be autumn and the colours would be as beautiful as ever, and Kashmir would go back to being a different Paradise.

The next disturbance would come late in 1989 but that was still far away.

She described Anantnag, home to ancient temples, Poonch with its seven lakes, Kishtwar with its pine and deodar trees, Kupwara with its meadows and valleys nearby, Sonamarg with its high mountains and its meadows of gold as the name suggested, its own valley of flowers and the nearby Gangbal Lake. She spoke of Aru Valley with its river of the same name, a tributary of the Lidder River, Khilanmarg on the way to Gulmarg, Gagangir and Kheer Bhawani.

The very names were evocative of Paradise, the photos and paintings established it incontrovertibly. It made Rajiv dream.

She also mentioned places from the other side—the other Kashmir—Walnut tree filled, with fields of Narcissus (Nargis) and Saffron, enthralling terrains, from her parents' memories. Valley after valley, each different, each splendiferous.

Skardu, with its beautiful architecture, its special sloping roofs ; Gilgit with its spectacular scenic beauty and peaches, apricots, pears; Hunza with its bubbling streams, luxuriant pastures; beautiful Nagar Valley (different from the also beautiful Naggar in Himachal where the Russian artist Roerich lived)—snow-capped mountains in the background.

There were photos also of adjoining Swat and its pleasing valleys and lakes, rushing rivers, slopes with flowers. Alexander's armies had been here, gardens in ancient Hindu epics were situated here, Buddhism flourished from before 500 BC for several centuries. There were stunning photos of Sharda and Neelam valleys, of the Baltistan valleys, of waterfalls, lakes, glaciers, torrents.

3

Rajiv's resolve since his last year of school—to focus on partying in general. He wasn't ready to have a single girlfriend and wanted to know and interact with many girls, experience that pleasure and richness.

'There's something about dancing with Indian women. When you put your arm around the waist or back, it is literally that,' thought Rajiv to himself at one of the many college parties that were on and not just on weekends. The sari doesn't cover the middle portion. Most of the time you don't think about it and put a perfunctory arm around.

Rajiv's mind went to the party sometime back which he had co-hosted with some other friends. Life had many good things—all the new music that kept coming from so many very creative groups, the pot, the Sexual and Cultural Revolution.

Everyone seemed to have had so much fun at the party—it could have belied expectations but didn't. Whenever they threw parties, all of the hosts liked to do a post mortem, especially if it seemed successful. There had been some interesting people at the party. Rajiv said he had met someone called Deepa and she had been intriguing. Nayantara said she had been waltzed off her feet by someone who had just joined the army. He held himself ramrod straight, clicked his heels and was dashing and elegant.

Ayesha had seemed to be in need of rescue from a fellow from Woodstock, situated in Landour, above Mussoorie. Rajiv cut in.

After some time, he was aware of his hand against her skin.

He felt her skin burning against his hand. He felt her other hand against his upturned hand. She was tall and *tres elegante*.

'I used to notice you taking the corners round the garden on your red bike,' she said.

'Yes, it would almost touch the ground,' he said.

'You were showing off,' she laughed.

She was wearing a matching sleeveless blouse with her sari. There was an irresistible urge to have contact with them. After some time, he switched his left hand to her shoulder. She seemed quite content to be guided like that. A continuous electric circuit started from her shoulder.

'Can you feel such sensuousness bordering on ecstasy through a shoulder?' he wondered. Had she any inkling of the sensations he was experiencing? If so, she didn't let on.

Vikramovarshiyam came to mind now. How much had happened with Urvashi's shoulder brushing Vikram's in the chariot in Kalidas' classic play.

It was yet another college party in Defence Colony. People were slow dancing or doing the shake or jiving or twisting skilfully. It looked good. One or two show offs did the Limbo Rock and went down horizontally almost to the floor. One of Rajiv's new friends from Lawrence School Sanawar, (pronounced Sanar by them) asked him who that vivacious looking girl at the other end of the room was. She's talking to that tall, fair guy. Rajiv's eyes fell on Ayesha.

'Oh, that's my sister's friend. She has come with us to the party.'

'Introduce me, yaar. She looks interesting.'

'This is a party. You don't need an intro. Go and ask her to dance,' said Rajiv, but did he feel a twinge of something?

4

Rajiv heard from a classmate that Joe was leaving late that night. It was already past dinner time.

It was one of those Delhi moonlit nights—the smell of night jasmine everywhere, as well as *chameli* and *champa*. All pervasive fragrance. Rajiv wanted to drop off a missive at Joe's. A farewell card. He would have to slip it under her door. Tiptoe in through the verandah and the garden, which her room overlooked. She was already asleep. Her parents' bedroom was on the other side. Her flight was that night very late as flights out of India generally were. He phoned Ayesha. His calls were not suspect. Best friend's brother. He asked if she could help him deliver a letter. Somehow, much better for a girl to be caught slipping in a note than a guy, if at all anyone has to be noticed. He would have done it on his own, he thought, but it was early enough to call Ayesha. The drive was beautiful; they delivered the letter. Rajiv felt full. He wanted the letter to reach that night. Their work done, there was leisure—there was no hurry. They drove. They chatted. They drove on that lovely road which wound past Jor Bagh towards Safdarjang's Tomb. They talked freely, of this and that, covered different topics that came to their heads. She said that men and women exchanges could not be defined. Could not be put into narrow or clear categories, labelled into boxes. They were very complex and far from clear cut. They always had potential.

They drove down the long and winding Ratendone Road. Mysterious turns. Unexpected surprises round the corner. They went back to the embassy area with wide avenues and broad boulevards. They kept driving. The night was young. They drove all over the beautiful moonlit city. Rajiv found his arm stretching to the back of her seat. He kept it there for a while. He found his arm gradually sliding southwards. It still wasn't touching her shoulder.

Neither of them wanted to go home. They drove and talked. His arm touched her shoulder. Just. It could be denied.

Rajiv didn't move his hand away from her shoulder. She didn't show any awareness of it. Gradually, the rest of his arm spread out over the back of the seat, slid down and was in contact with her back and shoulder more obviously. Nothing happened. They continued chatting normally. The beautiful city slid past at night—the roundabouts, the wide roads, the fountains, the canopy of trees, the sweet smell of night the pleasant graphite yellow lights. The Mughal monuments, the wide embassy area (with its promise of travel and lands to be visited in the future) slid past.

Rajiv talked of the potential of the human mind again, how many possibilities it had, how untapped its potential, what it was capable of and how little it had been realised.

Similarly, she said, 'The complexity, the non-definability of men and women relationships, how difficult and distorting it is to try to define them to always try to fit them into known relationships, into labels, into specific boxes or narrow set of drawers, whereas they at least overlapped, kept changing, moving, evolving like everything else in this world. It isn't brother and sister, boyfriend-girlfriend, husband-wife, cousins, friends of friends, etc. Often it is none of these things, it defies any text book social relationship, any classical and therefore more 'acceptable' and known social relationship. Often, it is pluralistic, it is something of many of these things or none of them. As soon as you tried to fit into anything it is already a distortion. Even if you just said 'friends' it is already a distortion. And what exactly does 'friends' mean between boys and girls and how long does it remain that, whatever that is?'

Rajiv took up the point—'If you said, "sister's friend", what does that mean? Is driving around on an errand, quite independent of and not even in the knowledge of my sister, part of it? Is there an independent relationship or only an indirect one of kinship? What are its do's and don'ts—or aren't there any? What are the social mores, the boundaries of the vaguer, socially more non-descript relationships?'

'These things are not even really clear within the more obvious and more defined relations,' she interrupted. 'And every usage of word describing such a relationship is quite inadequate and inaccurate, besides being static. If it falls between boxes or stools on top of that, what happens to any attempt to put boundaries around it or to describe it.'

Rajiv found the idea that she could think like this both exciting and appealing. She was sophisticated all right.

They had been driving around for a while now. They were nearing their neighbouring houses. The wide avenue was almost deserted. His arm was around her shoulder now. He leaned over and kissed her on the mouth.

5

Some afternoons after the drive around Ratendone Road, Rajiv was getting ready to shave in the bathroom of his bedroom downstairs. He liked this room because it was at one corner of the house and nearest to the gate. It was the best for quick getaway and the most accessible for numerous friends that kept dropping in. The bathroom had a door leading straight outside. It was a bit of a jump—the jamadarin came in from there as it was preferred she didn't enter the bathroom by way of the bedroom to clean the toilet.

Rajiv thought he heard Ayesha's voice outside at some distance. She must be going home from one of her visits to his sisters. He opened the bathroom door with the lather all over his face and said, 'Hi Ayesha.'

She said, 'Oh, hi,' and walked over and he automatically gave her a hand up to the bathroom. Despite wearing a sari, she managed. He was in his vest. Her glance at his shoulder somehow made him feel she had touched it.

They continued chatting while he lathered, shaved and splashed after- shave. She watched intently as he shaved. There was an intimacy to it. He brushed his teeth carefully and at different angles, as she stood pretty close to him and watched.

'Every time I shave or brush my teeth, especially in my bathroom, I'm still reminded of that time and her staring at me closely from so near,' he wrote in his journal, years later.

She went and sat on the very long sofa with pillow like upturned ends on either side, not far from the big bed in the centre of the room while he showered. He sat on the bed and put on his socks. The conversation continued. She seemed so attractive. There was a strong magnetic pull. He felt irresistibly pulled to the sofa. There was great gravitational force. He traversed the small gap between the bed and the sofa and kissed her on the lips. This was the second time in his life that he had kissed her.

'It was memorable. I can never forget it. It was like kissing someone I could never let go of. It was dallying with heaven'— his journal entry.

Her mouth opened partly. He sat bang next to her on the narrow space between her sari and the edge of the sofa and kissed her passionately. She kissed back and pulled his mouth with hers. There was a unique sucking sort of sound that was co-produced, pok-pok. They kept kissing. What had happened? After the brief encounter in the drive—that seemed such a long time back but actually was just a few days ago.

He detached himself with difficulty.

'You are tasting of soap,' she said. 'His eyes looked dreamy and more than half closed—Persian light brown eyes drunk with honey,' she thought. He had been very far away.

6

A bright, magical, silvery moonlight drenched the house and its hinterland. The terrace was full of moonlight. The evening was still young. Maybe he'd go to the disco. The Cellar had great music or one of the many others. There were a number of absorbing things to be continued. Rajiv would see.

He walked upstairs, with no particular purpose in mind, a glass of Coke with lots of ice tinkling in it. It could have been the most exotic or the most sophisticated drink for all the pleasure with which he held it. He walked down the upstairs gallery in no particular direction—vaguely towards the *chhat*—the terrace on which they'd slept many a moonlit summer night as children. Ah! Ayesha was over. She was talking animatedly at one end of the gallery to his sister. He walked over to them and joined in the conversation.

The Coke continued to tinkle in the glass. Everyone seemed very happy and they talked of this and that. After some time, he noticed to his surprise that his sister had vanished. Hey! She was the one talking in the first instance to Ayesha. He had just happened by. 'OK, she'll soon be back,' he thought. No matter. He kept chatting to Ayesha. They moved while conversing for some reason from the end of the gallery to the small verandah outside, overlooking the large terrace which was mostly open. She pointed to the stars and mentioned various constellations. He told her some of the names in Sanskrit—mangal, sapt rishi (the seven sages). It was magnificent. They stared at the moon. It did things to him. They moved closer whilst talking. No sign of his elusive sister. She seemed to have left them completely to their own devices. Suddenly, they were kissing. The kissing became more insistent.

They moved through an open door whilst still kissing, into the bedroom on the south side. There were beds there, neatly arranged in rows and columns. Rajiv and his siblings slept together in adjoining bedrooms along with their parents. They stood against each other in the corner and kissed, the Coke glass forgotten in the verandah.

Somebody might come in, that might be inconvenient. He ran down the corridor with her. She laughed at this continual shifting of ground. They ducked into a lesser used room.

Some visitors confessed when they felt more at ease to do so, that they felt spooky when they came to the house even in the long hot afternoons—when it was a *cirque du soleil* outside but dark inside.

The ghosts were a refuge. Hopefully, no one would peep into this darkened room. He manoeuvred her into the remotest corner and there they kissed, oblivious of the ghosts. He found his hands moving to her breasts diagonally under the blouse; they grew really big in his hands.

7

She often came over. A few days later, Rajiv thought: 'Let me see if she has come over.' She thought she didn't look nice with specs. He thought that the scholarly air or whatever her specs did to her made her more desirable, not less. She was attractive either way. Similarly, she thought, that having hair on her legs made her look less pleasing. They were as fetching—he tried to tell her but to no avail—got dismissed each time—'Oh, you won't understand.' 'But it's for us guys,' he thought. 'So, if our opinion doesn't count then whose does?'

There she was that golden afternoon, in an upstairs room with the sun streaming in, sitting at the top of the bed, reading a book. There was no one else in the room, all the doors were open; all these rooms had several entrances, covered only with chiks. There was none of the usual pre fore play conversation. He just entered the room from the far side, said, 'A,' and not even sure that she looked up, the book still in her hands, the specs still in place, kissed her full on the mouth. But Rajiv just did it, without any prelude, without so much as a by your leave, right in the middle of her reading—in mid-sentence. Ayesha allowed the kiss to take place. The kiss grew deeper and more intense, with his tongue exploring her mouth. So powerful was her kiss that everything stopped, including the heart, it seemed.

A bird called out in the distance. Any family member, anyone from the staff could have walked in any time. His parents didn't allow girlfriends but she wasn't even that. Heedless, they put everything into their mouth-to-mouth kissing, like people did those days. Nothing else mattered. Time stood still as it did at such moments. Life has moments, more than it has days.

Rajiv had heard Ayesha having discussions with his sister. She was already a feminist then. Capable of flying into a rage at perceived unequal treatment of women, not just at the general level, even in a personal situation.

'Why doesn't Navrekha's husband help her with looking after their baby?'

'Navrekha says he works very hard in the office.'

'How many times does he change the nappy? When the baby's crying at night, does he get up and walk her around, burp her?'

A couple of days later when she would come over for her daily visit to his sister, he asked her if she'd come for walk to nearby India Gate.

'Ayesha.'

'What's up?'

Rajiv said after a while, 'There are distinct sub cultures in our country. The norms and culture of different classes can be quite distinct and very different. Chowkidars and police constables often harass couples in parks, making out that it is indecent or immoral for them to be together, though it's the most natural thing in the world and the rest of it thinks so. Most of the time we live far removed from that in our own universe but we can suddenly come across it in situations like these. And then it's so strange. So alien for us that we get shocked in turn and don't quite know how to deal with it.'

'Are we on a date?' she asked suddenly.

'I don't know. You tell me. How could we be? I've never even asked you out in a date sense or taken you out formally ever. Besides, we are brother and sister, remember?'

'Are we?' she said and kissed him at the corner of his mouth.

'That was pretty incestuous,' Rajiv said laughing.

'Then what's this?' she asked as she kissed him impulsively, full on the mouth, there on the park bench... He closed his eyes. When he opened them, he saw her eyes, expressive, not dry but well lubricated with liquid, appealing, thoughtful.

Only the two of them knew about their kissing. Nothing would have been thought more improbable both in her house and his. She was the 'Secret Love' Doris Day sang about, except she didn't live at the other end of town.

When it happened one of the biggest elements was surprise—the unexpectedness, the craziness of it.

'But we were no different from anybody else in this respect and hardly expected it either but we'd kiss and wouldn't be able to tear ourselves away,'—his journal entry later.

In the distance they saw the figure of an approaching ruffian.

8

A bunch of them was going to see a Bergman film at a cine-club. Some friends of Rajiv's, his sister and some of her friends. They were all sitting in the car, waiting. It was getting late for the film. On top of that there was free seating.

Ayesha was over and was also coming. She hadn't come down from upstairs. They honked for her. Rajiv didn't know if some unacknowledged thought went through his head. He said he would go upstairs and fetch her.

She was in the bathroom adjoining the large sitting room next to the bedroom, where his sister hung out with her friends, especially before parties. There was a full-length mirror there; they used it as a dressing room and pre and post party hang out room. They chatted about their escapades and travails—*Little Women*. He knocked on the bathroom door. Ayesha opened it slightly and instead of saying she would be out shortly, she let him in. He caught a glimpse of her being kissed, in the mirror. It sent the blood rushing to his head. Very quickly their kiss escalated. There was no time to waste, everyone was waiting. Maybe that added to the urgency. But he doubted it, their kiss had its own urgency. He kissed her so hard that though she was kissing him back with equal urgency, she got pushed back. There was a chair in that bathroom. She got sat on it with the force of his seeking her.

Where was such passion coming from? He matched his mouth to hers and her cheeks went in and out with the alternate pulling and pushing now. Not too much time could have passed but all sense of it was lost. There was no time frame except for the very insistent honking from downstairs. They rushed downstairs. Said something. She gave him a reproachful look, seen only by him. People grumbled. They could have no idea of the earthquake they had been through and how drained they felt.

'This is the fifth time we have kissed,' he thought. 'We should stop counting or stop thinking it's nothing.' Maybe he wasn't yet ready to settle down. Maybe it didn't go with his image of sowing his wild oats but maybe this was it. These explosive casual encounters were getting to be something else.

That was how it had all started. One innocent kiss and then one thing led to another. It was mind blowing, where they'd started and how far they'd come.

This level of intimacy and contact had its emotional obverse. It was creating emotional attachments, bonds—that was in the nature of the thing—whether they were aware of it or not, whether they consciously wanted it or not.

Was this leading to love—beyond desire?

He hadn't been willing to acknowledge a desire which smacked of incest towards someone who had grown up with them. Was this sublimated desire, at least, partly? Did it exist in its own right?

This was all forbidden territory. It was time to be clear about this brother-sister thing.

The next day he bumped into her about to ascend the staircase. It was tea time.

'Ayesha?'

'Uh-huh.'

'You remember the badminton game we had ages back?'

'We used to play often.'

The sun was setting—the sky was filled with a myriad colours; yellow and gold, crimson and pink on shades of blue and white. It was stunning, as breath-taking as Ayesha's kiss.

Shall we have a quick match before you go up? She looked at her watch—she could still make tea.

It was hot; she took off her T-shirt. She was playing in her lace vest. Her skin peeped through the net. Her gold-coloured shoulders glowed in the light. They shone because of their own luminosity, the evening light and her sweat. It was a memorable image.

After a few points, Rajiv crossed over to her side of the net and took her in his arms. Initially, she was startled but allowed herself to be kissed. They closed their eyes. Ayesha felt she was transported far away, over the rainbow—she didn't know a kiss had such potential.

Shakily, they resumed the game. Rajiv's hand was far from steady as he served.

'Let's put some spirit, some fire in the competition.'

'Oh, in the competition…' she teased.

'C'mon, c'mon, let's play.'

His mind wasn't on the game; she was hitting well. She shot ahead. He tried to catch up and started hitting shots in his impatience—disastrous!

She won.

'OK, what'll it be?' he said resignedly, resting on the grass and drinking some fresh lime.

'I'll pass,' she said mischievously, a twinkle in her eye.

'No, you won, I'll get you a present.'

'Come here,' she said.

He went close to her.

'This is what I want,' she said, bold and beautiful, and kissed him, their mouths going smack.

'You know,' he said, 'that match was a lot closer than the score suggests.'

'A lot tougher too,' she said.

Through the kiss he thought, 'I can't live without kissing this girl.'

'What does that mean?'

'I can't live without her—her charm, her unique mannerisms.'

'This is the sort of kiss that results in love making. You can only kiss someone like that if you…'

'Hey, whoa, Jones it's only me!' she said, interrupting his thoughts.

He tried to say something—welling up within him.

'A …'

Ayesha was not immune to jealousy. More of emotional interaction than of any perceived physical transgression. Rajiv felt it when he was laughing and talking with a vivacious girl who had been chosen Miss LSR at one of the best colleges in Delhi.

Or when he had gone to see a French movie at the Alliance Francaise and had sat next to his young and attractive French teacher.

Nor was Rajiv. Ayesha could be outrageously flirtatious. Impetuous Ayesha.

A few afternoons later, Rajiv came from behind as she was absorbed in her book. But she was quick. She turned her head backwards and kissed him.

'You were going to do that anyway,' she laughed.

'Am I getting so predictable?' he said in mock grumble.

But the kiss was too tempting to indulge in banter. They didn't want to let go, their bodies remained motionless, locked in a passionate kiss. Her mouth got pulled in and out with his kiss.

Everything went into our kisses and it was what made Life so worthwhile and its fabric and texture immediately rich, *surtout*, the emotions were too powerful not to be shared. —Rajiv wrote in his diary afterwards.

They settled down to long contented kissing. It throbbed and pulsated in a steady flow, like very slow love making. They experimented with different ways of kissing. They kissed closed lips on closed lips. Then his mouth was inside hers, while she kissed and the outside.

There was no ending point which was part of the charm, that elusive sense of forever and the sense of freedom.

A couple of afternoons later, she came and sat serenely at the other end of the room. He put the old brass chitkani up. It always made a sound going up. She lay down gracefully on the sofa. The sofa in Rajiv's room was tailor made for kissing. Ayesha could stretch her legs. Its raised ends were comfortable, like pillows. It was very long and narrow. He could lie right next to her as they kissed. Its green colour was soothing. They held hands as they kissed, with her wedged between him and the rising side of the sofa, one of her sophisticated, elegant saris blowing with the wind of the fan and exposing her legs. She kept smoothening it down. As they kissed and the kiss became more open, he found his hand going under the sari and up her legs. Her legs so forbidden, so secret, so full of mystery, covered by the sari. Some days ago, he had put his hand under her sari and she had interrupted their kissing to shake her head. 'You don't want me to?' he had asked. That day again his impulse took him there. Often, the best things happen spontaneously. She didn't stop him. Perhaps she knew that he intended thus far and no more.

Her thighs were together and his hand under the sari on top of them caressed the upper thighs. It rested on the crest of where they met. It cupped both. He kept his palms *contre* the smoothness of her thighs. Her light golden thighs were soft. They were cool, yet his hands sizzled. It moved gently down one inner thigh and very slowly up the other thigh, felt the delicate contours. With both his hands on her thighs, he kissed her. Double ecstasy.

'When I was a child and watched Hollywood movies in the '50s and early '60s and saw it in the pictures of passionate kisses in film mags and covers of books, I saw how much was put into the kiss. Everything,' Rajiv said to Ayesha, when they paused.

'Yes,' she agreed, 'lovemaking (unlike the current '60s sexual revolution) was not really on, especially not as an almost immediate sequel to kissing. Lovemaking without a romantic involvement/commitment was inconceivable and prior to marriage often difficult. In the courtship everything had to be given to the kiss.'

'It, therefore, got the richness it deserved. The kiss, far from being "only" a kiss, is in many ways more intimate and personal than other forms of lovemaking, including intercourse,' Rajiv continued.

Things were moving fast with Ayesha.

She came swimming a few days later; a bunch of friends were playing water polo. There was considerable jostling for the ball. She was in the opposing team. The ball went to her; Rajiv tackled her. They fought for control of the ball in the deep end. He was very close to her. He found his legs drifting towards her, crossing her legs with the natural push of the water. The intertwining lasted as long as the fight for the ball continued.

They lingered after both teams had gone in to change. It was very dark now. The pool attendant had vanished.

The rain pouring down from the dark clouds above felt pleasantly cooler. Rajiv had tactical advantage in underwater swimming. He followed her deep underwater and managed to grab her. 'Hey!' she said, as she slipped away. They were both laughing once again but there was an undercurrent, a sexual tension in it now, though that's not how they had started out that evening. His arms went around her wet back, holding her from getting away. He managed to intertwine his legs with hers. The touch of her inner thighs made his mind reel. 'What's this, Charles?' she enquired mockingly, her eyes twinkling in mischief, disarmingly cocking her head slightly to one side. She was charm itself. He let her go as they swam together towards the shallow. 'And what now, Charles?' she said, audacious. He went up close to her. He kissed her on the mouth.

After a brief kiss she drew back in the water, her thighs still touching his. She sensed his playfulness and became even more so, continually slipping out of his hands.

She let herself be kissed for a while, swimming costume against swimming costume. The kiss became more passionate with the rain completely enveloping them, unmindful of all else, in the privacy it gave them. The thought that it was *her* still wildly excited Rajiv.

Their cheeks drew back in concentric circles. Rajiv thought— 'Gosh, what on earth is happening? I better stop'—but just couldn't. 'Just a little longer,' he thought. A strand of her hair fell along her cheek and came into their mouths. They let it stay there. It was too urgent to be interrupted. They looked at each other through soft eyes. Rajiv's expression said—'Whew! What was that?'

When they paused Rajiv kept his thighs locked with hers and then neither of them could bear the disuniting and started again with no let up in the passion. No doubt the rain, the Pool, her skimpy beach volleyball type costume, the touch, the feel of her wet body were factors; he wrote subsequently—'Gosh, I really lost my head.'

As they spent more time together, they discovered that he was as tidy as she was not. She seemed to revel in a symphony of disarray. It wasn't conscious. Her manner was charming, the result often inconvenient. She didn't share Rajiv's love of sport but she enjoyed swimming and badminton.

Rajiv lived in a world of the Folk, Pop, Rock music of the times. Something would be playing on his record changer or in his head. Some of the very catchy songs were in the form of 45s. But you could stack them up to 8 and they would keep falling down on to the turntable in turns. '60s music had to be played loudly. Ayesha enjoyed it but it wasn't so essential for her. For Western classical music, it was the same story, but she in turn was won over when she witnessed Rajiv sometimes listening to Chopin or Debussy, entranced.

Their days were studded with 'Strangers In The Night'[9], 'These Boots Are Made For Walkin''[10], 'The Sound of Silence'[11], 'Black is Black'[12], 'Monday, Monday'[13], 'Summer in the City' [14]

The Swinging Sixties had already produced *Pierrot le Fou* with Belmondo, *Belle de Jour* with Catherine Deneuve, *Blow Up* and *Alfie*.

Rajiv had loved Bernard Malamud's *The Fixer*. It was the time of *Rosencrantz and Guildenstern Are Dead* and Elia Kazan's *The Arrangement*.

It was the time of the mini skirt debuting in King's Road, Chelsea, attitudes to sex fundamentally changing and Vietnam War protests with legendary folk singers prominent. It was the time of Tariq Ali, President of the Oxford Union and British student leader.

9

As the relationship evolved, Rajiv impulsively suggested that they go to the Pink City. He had never seen Jaipur. The two of them could hardly go alone. She told her parents that she was going with a friend from the hostel, Sue, who agreed to cover for her. They knew that girl well and liked her. Ayesha's father knew someone and they got a good off-season rate at one of the Palace Hotels there with very large, stately gardens next to each wing.

Ayesha wore one of her exquisite saris with their graceful colours and texture. They went to the centuries old Amber Fort on the outskirts of the beautiful city. The drive into and out of the city witnessed high fort walls, majestic gateways, hill plateaus on both sides. Dramatic. 'What an entrance and an exit,' said Ayesha.

Amber was steeped in atmosphere and history. One was transported to another time, another era. Its ancient bricks, walls, archways, steps spoke their antiquity.

There were several levels in the fort and its parameter walls. There were also portions of the Fort from which one could get an excellent view of other parts—archways which gave fantastic views, verandahs which looked down just a level or two below—an architect's delight. This effect was enhanced by some of the parts being in a state of disrepair. Some parts were just ruins. Ayesha and Rajiv discovered that, unintentionally, they were playing hide and seek. One of them would linger to marvel at something or look at the now setting sun in the distance with its shades of orange, pink and red, with slices of a light sky blue here and there. Then one would be just a few steps away but around a wall or an archway or a bend in the step or just at such an angle that the other one would seem lost. Or very near but at a different level. She would be hidden from view and could easily have wandered far while Rajiv was lost in his thoughts, transported to another time, and then suddenly round a corner he would see the colour of her sari, her eyes so beautiful, so expressive.

As they climbed up, they held hands from time to time or their hands brushed against each other's. He waited round a turn in the steps at one place inside the Fort—it was totally dark there, there seemed the possibility of bats. Just as she turned it, he stole a kiss.

'Hey!' she said, breathless and taken by surprise. 'Incorrigible.'

Another time they were high up in the Fort, in a *chhatri* structure typical of Hindu architecture, open on all four sides with a curved temple like roof and pillars. Much of the Fort could be seen below and the plains far away strewn with rocks. As she was looking out with the sun on her face and the 'dark gogs' making her look smart, Rajiv wondered how come he hadn't noticed her before. The unexpected hideways, portals access—leading to the other side—the many levels added to possibilities and to surprise.

It was early summer and the nights were cool and moon drenched. Everything was bathed in a silvery light. Ayesha and Rajiv went for a walk in one of the gardens. There was a gateway leading to another enclosure. They entered and saw a garden full of marble statues, some of them not well kept. They must have looked beautiful during the day but as they entered that enclosure, suddenly there was an eerie feeling—as if these were ghostly figures standing in rows and columns in that enclosure. That feeling was confined to that enclosure but distinct. They shivered and withdrew. Rajiv's house wasn't the only haunted place.

As soon as one left it, it was once again a beautiful palace garden steeped in history and romance. There were Persian style bushes, shaped like peacock feathers, peacocks walking about, beautiful architecture and space. The Hotel had very large, stately rooms all overlooking a quad or a garden. The dining room had chandeliers and lead to a pillared verandah—much like Rajiv's house—which then opened on to a garden. The lobby, the lounge, the bar were all brightly lit and plush.

In the verandah adjoining the hotel room, they sat on adjoining chairs with arm rests. Their arms were along each other's but their bodies didn't touch much. They didn't need to; their mouths were riveted on to each other's.

A leaf drifted slowly down by the window. A light breeze stirred outside. It was another heavenly night. Light blue made silvery by moonlight. The colour of the night.

The next afternoon after the fort visit, the pre-Afternoon tea kisses from Delhi intensified into French kissing. Their mouths swelled up like freshly filled phulkas, fitting perfectly. The cross suction held their mouths together. They couldn't be prised open.

As their osculation escalated, their cheeks got pinched in with the force of the kiss. So great the desire, their kisses became tunnel kisses. Then cascaded into a narrow tunnel joined at the mouth. This might be replicating above what might happen below one day, if they ever got that far, though in a way, this was more intimate.

No distinguishable boundary remained as their mouths melted into one. It made them perspire with beads of sweat on their backs, brows and upper lips.

That was where it had started, it was the beginning and

the end point. They stayed like that for a long time, changing positions in the osculation. They had already become experts in kissing each other.

From time to time, he opened his eyes and looked at her beautiful face next to his and the lovely hue of gold on her face.

'I find her irresistible. I cannot imagine ever getting tired her. The very thought of her, her very name excites me,' he scribbled in his diary.

Various other people that there had been close encounters with floated through his mind. Maybe women forgot people more easily once it was over. Close sexual encounters even when they had been primarily that, had their continuing emotional impact. It was the obverse of the same thing, the urge to label just being an inadequate human attempt to understand, partly through simplification.

After their own disbelief and the initial surprise of family and friends, Rajiv and Ayesha became a pair.

All times of the day and all seasons were beautiful. The sunlight was dappled under the thick trees. It made Patterns on the walls like those in the song by Simon and Garfunkel.

The leaves from the silk cotton tree floated down, as did the cotton in the breeze. At the other end of the garden was its cousin. A tall tree that grew outside the bedroom window from just a handful of seeds to past the skylight and beyond the top of the house. With its many branches and thick foliage reaching the skies, it reminded Rajiv of *Jack and the Beanstalk*.

They listened to 'A Whiter Shade of Pale', 'Groovin'' and 'California Dreamin''.

They went to plays and discotheques, to films and cultural events; at parties they were a couple, though they danced with others.

Delhi in the winter, with its crisp blue sky, radiant golden sunshine filled up every space. It made even the leaves sparkle, lit the bushes and the light beige bark of the tall trees. Yet the breeze was quite strong and cold. It made them shiver even in the day.

The women with colourful shawls and saris, salwar kameezzes. Indian girls—laughing, smiling, vivacious, clever, intelligent, gracious, sophisticated, flirtatious, modern, pot smoking—the prettiest in the world. But when you fell in love with someone, where did nationality come in?

The weeks and months flew.

He was in love with Ayesha. There could be no doubt about it.

Sgt. Pepper's came out. It felt like the apotheosis of The Beatles' incredible creativity. There was nowhere else to go after this. Each song was so special. 'What would you do if I sang out of tune, would you get up and walk out one me?' Or '… Dragged a comb across my head, made the bus in seconds flat… somebody spoke and I went into a dream…'

Rajiv and his friends lay down, smoked pot and listened to them. Everything got heightened, the sound of the Cicada, the drop falling from one leaf on to another.

The Six-Day War took place. It caught the popular imagination in India. A lone State fighting so many countries ganged up against it. For its right to exist. There was admiration. In the press, in discussions it wasn't seen as a pro or anti-Muslim thing, nor in terms of political correctness or otherwise. The official line did not reflect this. They didn't want to upset so many Arab countries.

Rajiv had no inkling that things were going to start falling apart and his world would come crashing down.

10

Ayesha's grandfather passed away of cardiac arrest. He had had no history. He was in his 60s, strong as an ox and in very good shape.

The family used all their contacts to be allowed to visit the other side. Indian-Muslims were still allowed to migrate to Pakistan—move bag and baggage if certain conditions were fulfilled, like having close relatives there. During the mayhem of the sudden partition, it was enough to be Muslim or Hindu to move to the other side.

'Rajiv,' she said suddenly, as the days merged into one another like dreams. 'I may have to go.'

Rajiv raised a quizzical eyebrow, thinking that this was one of Ayesha's indecipherable thoughts.

'My grandfather has passed away on the other side of Kashmir and my bua and grandmother can't manage. We have vast Estate and interests over there, much more than we have on this side. More importantly, it's a matter of family duty, care.'

A long silence, while this was digested.

'How long will you go for? How will you come and go? It's not all that easy. In fact, I imagine it's very tough, if not impossible.'

Another silence.

'I don't know. My family is making it sound like it may be for good. We don't know if we'll be able to get across. There are formidable barriers on both sides. But if we do, as you yourself said, we can't just come and go.

'Besides, our friends in Kashmir are full of tales of how well Muslims who chose to go to Pakistan after Partition, have done. They are helped by the government there, they are given cash subsidies and generous loans, they are given ownership of land to start a business, and other friends help them to set up, in more ways than one.'

The sky was falling.

'You are not serious. You can't just up and go. You are Indian, like me. What about your studies, your life here, your friends? You have grown up here, Ayesha. You don't know any other life. You are truly from here. What will you do there? Where and how will you continue your studies?'

'Anyway, Rajiv, it's come up and won't go away. I thought I'd better tell you.'

'It's a very big decision. We, my family, realise that. It has enormous consequences for us. But sometimes you come to these moments in life, when you have to choose, to decide. And these moments come without warning.'

'I have fallen for you, Ayesha, though we didn't start off like that.'

'Accidental lovers,' she smiled.

'We fell into it.'

The topic came up every day in Ayesha's home. It would have to be decided and not in much time, its unexpectedness and suddenness notwithstanding.

It was the toughest decision of Wajahat's life but he resigned. The family had incontrovertible credentials for going to the other side of Kashmir. They crossed over into land that did not seem any different except for the political hues given by man. They were met on the other side by a civil service functionary and his long-lost family.

He was careful that his decision not be portrayed as a defection, nor politicised.

Wajahat was from an old Kashmiri family and was well liked amongst the ordinary Kashmiris. They could look up to him—he represented the best of their self-image. He was tall and Kashmiri fair, one of the MPs that worked hard in his constituency and did not get mixed up in populism.

His relations with the central and state government establishments remained excellent. When he left, he did not burn bridges and everyone understood. If ever the larger situation changed, there would be no barriers to his return.

Once the decision to leave was taken, arrangements took a long time. The whole life of the family had to be uprooted and transplanted. The smallest aspect was made doubly difficult because they were dealing across a hostile border.

They would leave after Ayesha's IInd Year college Exams got over. One more year and she would have got her BA (Honours). By the time they left it was July. He thought he would always have Ayesha.

The drama of the beautiful Monsoons had started. It could be exceptionally dark in the middle of the afternoon, it would rain so hard it would be difficult to do anything else, one could only stand and look at it. There are times in life when one has to let go and allow oneself time to stand and stare, as the poet wrote. It would produce vivid sunsets full of extraordinary hues that only God's palette could produce. The sky would be so clear and washed, the stars at night so luminous after the downpour.

Term would be starting. Everybody else would be going back to college. The college quads would have the special smell of neem trees. Ayesha would be going to another life, leaving her friends, the only life she had known, behind.

They worked at making sure that she would get credit on the

other side, at least for the two years she had completed. She was highly intelligent, they knew, but that doesn't always get reflected in marks. Fortunately, in her case it did. For the nth time, they wondered, despite being in the government themselves, as to why the Education Ministry had not worked at getting equivalences for Indian degrees internationally, a matter of prime importance as more and more students chose to study abroad and suffered because of their BAs not being recognised in America.

Their government network made a big difference but despite all the attestation from the Indian side, Wajahat's sister and mom had to make it happen on the Pakistani Kashmiri side. Ayesha couldn't repeat two years. The quality of her education had been very good.

Wajahat, his wife and daughter, all wondered several times whether there was any other way out other than this extreme step of shifting lives. Had there been easy ingress and egress it would not have seemed so drastic, so irreversible. But this was not a case of neighbours like France and Belgium or Sweden and Denmark.

There was the inevitable pain of departure, of parting, of leaving behind the life they had mostly known.

In the final analysis, Wajahat couldn't abandon his mother and sister and the extensive ancestral land that had been with the family for generations. That too was home. Two compelling domiciles but it had to be one due to political reasons. Home is where the heart is, but what if the heart belongs to two nearby places that were part of one?

If the West and Communist East were divided by the Iron Curtain, this was something even more impenetrable.

The days before their parting, Ayesha and Rajiv could not bear to eat. They picked at their food if they came to a meal at all.

They held hands, talked and when they kissed it was tinged with the parting round the corner. They could no longer lose themselves in it. Time, instead of stopping, was ever present.

She looked at him long on the final day at the airport, a look that went straight to the heart and communicated many things. There was nothing more to be said. He stood at the fence which separated the civil aerodrome building from the tarmac. Visitors could come right to where passengers actually walked to the plane to climb its stairs.

She promised to write but they both knew that the letters would not reach. Trunk calls through a telephone operator was not a possibility. An international trunk call through an operator for six minutes could be booked for England, but between the two neighbours, not really. So near and yet so far.

There was joy at the reunion with that part of the family, mixed with grief at the loss that enabled it.

Rajiv thought about Ayesha.

'Every place I go I think of you...

Every song I sing I sing to you...'

'Leaving on a Jet Plane.'

How to even attempt to explain what happened between them? Words, language were so inadequate—maybe so were even thoughts. Why did everything have to be put into words? Described? Understood? Human need?

The pleasure of shared time, the sweetness of memories, nothing would take that away. The joy of having known her and loved her. The Lovin' Spoonful sang about some of this magic.

'Love is a many splendored thing.'

Whatever turns life took, whatever its vicissitudes, Rajiv believed that he would always have Ayesha who had grown up with him here. But she'd gone now, though part of him found it hard to believe.

The void of her absence and of knowing that I will probably never see her again—Rajiv wrote in his diary. When I see the chlorophyll in the leaves, the wind rustling the tall trees in our garden and on the wide boulevards, when I look at the unbelievable, incommunicable blue of the sky from the upstairs window, my heart is filled with an unmistakable longing. I will probably never see her again, not in this Life. And in some other form, if we both come back, will it matter? These times with her have been enraptured. When I hear any of our songs, my heart misses a beat.

It was over now. So how to deal with the feeling that comes up when I see the blue sky etched with gold?

11

Rajiv could hardly eat for several days after Ayesha left. The womenfolk in the family worried about him.

He went back to College. But he had no mental space for anything. He was far away. Honours required attention in class and daily revision. The formulae needed practice and clear comprehension of the methodology.

The Standard Deviation and the difference between Mean, Median and Mode that they had studied at the beginning of First Year Statistics seemed distant. A few good friends took turns doing proxy for him when attendance was called and he was missing. They changed their voices and projected them. The Professor, in a hurry to get on with the lecture, did not look up.

Very gradually, he started to feel a little better in the general bonhomie of College and the party scene, though he missed her terribly. He went back to Shakespeare Society auditions held in the Staff Room in the afternoons, when it was empty, and focussed on reading well and projecting his voice from the stomach, though his mind wasn't fully there.

'The lazy hazy crazy days of summer' turned to Autumn and then to *Deezember*, a la Maurice Chevalier.

Dr Christiaan Barnard did the first heart transplant in South Africa.

Catherine

1

It was the summer of 1968. Simon and Garfunkel came out with 'Bookends', Sly and the Family Stone with 'Dance to the Music' and The Mamas & The Papas had been releasing beautiful songs one after the other.

The IIIrd year exams had just ended for Rajiv... In a couple of months, it would be the Monsoons in Delhi. Ayesha had left in July the previous year. He had to get over it. The late '60s were a heady time and he was very young.

India followed the British system of three years in University for a BA, unlike the American four years of undergraduate work after school. Indian students, when they went abroad for studies, increasingly preferred American Universities to British ones, unlike the pre-Independence years or the '50s. So, there was a mismatch.

Rajiv too would have to do one more year of undergrad work because of the four-year American BA, although he would get a BA from Delhi.

The American Field Service, with its office in New York, was very active in those days. Its exchange programs brought students from all over the States to stay with families in various states of India. These turned out to be upper middle-class students. Maybe those were the ones that applied, were interested or knew about it. One such student, Catherine, tall, lissom, beautiful, was staying with friends of Rajiv's in Golf Links in a large house overlooking the park. To Rajiv, Golf Links seemed to be full of pretty girls. It held the promise of meeting them at parties. These students were here for almost three months. The Field Service Exchange students were mostly from private schools which ended the school year a couple of weeks earlier than the public schools. The final exam was normally about a month before school closed and these schools usually granted permission to Exchange students do a special project elsewhere after that, with something well thought of like the American Field Service.

There was a warm up party the very first evening where the Indian hosts in every city, in this case Delhi, invited the visiting Exchange Students with their hosts and some friends. Aparna, the daughter of the house, had met Rajiv at several parties which were essentially dance parties, and enjoyed dancing with him. He was one of the first friends she thought of when planning this party.

It was a classic. Some enchanted evening sort of setting. Rajiv felt an inexplicable pain. She was standing in a group of four.

Catherine also saw him looking at her from across the room.

He went and joined the group. The other three were young fresh-faced American boys. Don, Dean and Alfred. Don and Dean were brothers from Mount Kisco in New York. Don was very tall already. Alfred was from Brooklyn. They were planning to go to Yale and Cornell respectively. Catherine's destination was Mount Holyoke. She also had admission at UC Berkeley.

'I think your country is fascinating,' all three of them said almost at once. Rajiv suppressed a smile.

Alfred moved on to another group. He was here to mix. Dan followed soon thereafter. They were both very personable and Rajiv found himself liking them. He found himself hanging out with them in the days that followed before he ended up spending more and more time with Catherine. They played Tennis together and talked easily about girls. How free and easy America sounded about boys and girls mixing. He would go there one day. Maybe settle down there. Life there sounded like so much fun.

Rajiv fell easily into conversation and she forgot that she was elsewhere. Her first evening was going to be a very pleasant one. She found the accent charming—close to the English but without the aspirating of the Ps and the Ts.

She talked about her hobbies, her plans, subjects she liked, the films and Sports she liked. She drew a blank with the TV shows. They were not available in India but the films came with great fanfare to the local movie halls.

The party spilled on to the verandah. As the evening darkened the stars brightened.

The music system was playing 'Bus Stop' by The Hollies. Rajiv asked Catherine to dance. He guided her smoothly in the already filling up dance floor. 'On a Carousel' came on. It was beautiful music and the system was excellent. It was difficult not to get caught up in it and to lose oneself in it.

'I'm Happy Just To Dance With You' from *A Hard Day's Night* came to his head.

Rajiv discovered that unlike people in India, who were equally familiar with both American and British music, the Americans had only heard some of the top British singers who, for whatever reason, had made it across the pond. Cliff Richard whose 'Living Doll', 'The Young Ones', 'Constantly', to name a few, were adored in India, was unknown in transatlantic quarters.

As if to make a point:

> 'When the girl in your arms,
> Is the girl in your heart,
> Then you have got everything
> You're as rich as a King.

So hold her tight,
And never let her go...', came on.

There were Japanese magic lanterns in the verandah. Rajiv glided her in between them.

'Have you read *Le Petit Prince* by Antoine St Exupery?' he asked her. She had. In French. He pointed up at one of the brightly luminous stars. It twinkled in recognition. 'That's the planet of the Petit Prince. Maybe he will appear again one day.'

She smiled with a tinge of sadness. 'We'll have to go to the middle of the Sahara for that,' she said.

They sat down on chairs next to potted plants, shaded by a screen. The lamp there created a particular golden light. It created a sense of intimacy. Other people came and joined them, including some of the American Field Service boys and girls, and then drifted away. They seemed absorbed in each other, noticed the presence of others less and less. Others noticed the intensity too. Something was happening, as it can happen only amongst the very young and innocent. It seemed magical, contagious. For Rajiv, there was also the feeling of conquest and the high that comes from it.

Even if nothing else happened, Catherine would not forget this evening, these moments. The grandfather clock in the next room chimed midnight then 1 a.m. Time took wings and seemed irrelevant.

Catherine came with an open mind, when she decided to come with the Field Service to a country as far away and with such a unique culture as India. She didn't know what to expect. A beau was not one of them. Can the role of chance ever be underestimated? Or is the incipient possibility there oftener than we care to acknowledge?

But—there it is—she wrote to her friends. Her friends learnt that he was handsome, charming, sophisticated.

Catherine asked him if he could help her with some Math the next day around tea time. She was entertained by the concept of tea in the early evening. Didn't exist in America. Rajiv found the Maths very easy but he found it hard not to be distracted by her presence. The Golf Links sky started acquiring various shades of pink and auburn. The future was filled with possibilities. Catherine absentmindedly kept putting one end of a yellow pencil in her mouth as she worked. This was very appealing. A fleeting thought came to Rajiv—he wanted to be that pencil. She had tied her blonde hair in two plaits at either end. Her hazel eyes were deep, expressive, her smile charming, her laughter and humour infectious. She went out of the room briefly. Rajiv quickly put that end of the pencil in his mouth. Odd that it tasted only like a pencil. When she came back, she put it in her mouth again in an absorbed sort of way.

He asked her out the next day. Did she have any engagement? There was a production of Chekhov's *The Seagull* by Yatrik in an open-air theatre in the Exhibition Grounds. Would she like to come for that?

Catherine looked enquiringly at her hosts. 'Sure,' they said, 'go.'

He picked her up in a Fiat 1100 which had the pick-up of an Alfa Romeo. The play was well enacted and stimulating.

After the performance they ended up at a marble table in the 24-hour Coffee Shop at The Oberoi. It had a special ambience. Charming. There were many layers of culture in India. It felt congruous. It was quite near the performance. It was so easy to chat to her. When they reached her house, it became obvious to both that they didn't want the evening to end. She called him into the room, which had a direct entrance from the verandah, bathed in moonlight. The house was in darkness, everyone was sleeping. There was an unspoken understanding. It seemed a perfectly natural continuation.

He sat behind her and put both arms loosely around her neck. They looked out into the night. There was an inexorable quality to it. The words flowed intermittently. They were self-aware enough to know that they were very young. What would he do when she left?

Whatever happened, neither of them would forget that night in which nothing happened and so much happened. Could he put into words what they felt that whole night? He didn't think so. Except the inexplicable intensity he felt. He could see she felt it too.

Strange can be the chemistry between a man and a woman. *Toujours imprevisible.*

When he stepped out of the room there was the very early morning breeze.

Next day was a Sunday and there were Sunday morning jam sessions at many restaurants. He took her to La Cabana in South Extension. The music was very danceable and Rajiv found delicious beads of perspiration forming on his brow. Evening there was a party he wanted to take her to.

'Whoa,' she said, 'do I get to meet anybody else, do anything else in Delhi?' she asked, smiling.

'One of my designations is ABW. I should put it on my business card. Adviser to Beautiful Women. I am told by many a lady friend that I have an eye for clothes. India has fantastic Textiles and not just silk, exquisite handicrafts from Kashmir and elsewhere. Let me take you to Cottage Industries Emporium. It has good stuff and the prices are government controlled. Shopping is a must do in your visit. And then we can eat in Bankura, it's charming, cheap and unpretentious, with tasty food and good service.'

Don, Dean and Alfred dropped by for a game of tennis. They all got totally absorbed in the game and Rajiv was thrilled with his placements. In the volleying, he would aim for the face of whoever was standing at the net, wearing dark glasses and grinning. Afterwards, they all lay sprawled, revelling in the smell of freshly cut grass mixed with the sweat of achievement.

'You seem very taken with Catherine,' Don ventured. A look of rapture crossed Rajiv's face. He tried to hide it but it was lost on none. They smiled in empathy. There was still time for the visit and they were all very young. Their lives lay ahead of them, anything was possible.

All the AFS students were strangers to each other. They had met for the first time in India. Catherine had little time to get close to anyone. All her time was being spent with Rajiv. College life meant parties every day. The notion of just Friday night and Saturday night were laughable—not for the happening set. And since this was the late '60s, there was lots of creative new music coming out every day. New groups all the time from all over. Mireille Mathieu, Charles Aznavour, and above all, Francoise Hardy from across the Channel, to name but a few. Peter and Gordon, The Yardbirds, The New Faces, Herman's Hermits, Deep Purple—as part of a beautiful creative outpouring, on both sides of the Atlantic, all at the same time. This translated into night after night of music to swing to, to get high on. She wrote to two of her best friends. They got a sense of how intensely she was beginning to feel and how fast it was happening. They got a fragrance of the moonlit nights and the night jasmine, the nights spent dancing. They felt the headiness. They were pleased for their batchmate but also wondered what next.

After her initial protest, Catherine had started seeing more and more of Rajiv. He took her to lunch at the pool side restaurant at The Oberoi.

He proposed a swim at Ashoka. She had to go somewhere with her hosts but she could come later.

The pool at Ashoka Hotel was lovely, the water was always a deep aquamarine blue. It was shaped like an irregular two-thirds of a circle, with especially rounded curves at either end. It gave one a sense of not knowing where the pool went. There was a balcony at the top not far above the pool. One could easily have dived from it into the pool, except that it was fenced off with a designed balcony boundary. It was attached to the 24-hour coffee shop and there were usually people at tables enjoying the view of the pool on either side and the vast expanse of garden next to it, set back from the engaging Indo-Saracenic style architecture of the Hotel. The pool went below the overhang of the balcony, providing a private area underneath and cutting off the view of one side of the pool from the other side. They changed, grabbed the blue and white striped towels, and jumped in. There was not a soul around in the late afternoon haze. Catherine swam away from Rajiv, laughing. She was a very fast swimmer, quick and agile, her long, slender legs kicking strongly.

He chased her in the pool. It led to their first kiss under the overhang.

Over the course of the next few days, they talked about their dreams, their plans, their growing up, their schools, their siblings, their friends, their romantic encounters. What did she want to be, to do in life. She didn't know yet. Everything was possible right now.

The answer would emerge over time. Her heart would tell her. 'Go where you wanna go, do what you wanna do', The Mamas & The Papas sang.

When it had been time for applications the previous year, Rajiv had chosen America over Europe and England. He had been attracted to the America of those years. Rajiv hadn't wanted to do another undergraduate degree. He had toyed with the idea of doing an MA Previous in Delhi University and then going straight for a Masters to the US, but had finally decided to go straight after graduation.

Rajiv had been strongly attracted by the liberal, counter culture credentials of UC Berkeley, combined with its high academic reputation. The fees were also much lower for foreign students than at some of the Ivy League Universities on the East Coast, where he had also applied. It helped that it was a State University. He tried but scholarships for undergrad work were really difficult.

Catherine was aware of her beauty and attractiveness but not self-conscious. Her peers thought highly of her intelligence but she put in enough work to do well in class. She liked people, parties and dancing. In the cultural changes sweeping America in the '60s, she was one of the first to smoke weed, put on eye catching psychedelic clothes and take part in sit-ins.

Rajiv taught her yoga. She had heard about it but not practiced it till now. His parents had got him and his siblings a teacher in High School. He was a good teacher and they all grew to enjoy it. 'Breathing is the most important part of it,' he told her. Yoga was the joining of breathing with body postures and stretching in various ways. It wasn't a showy off, though accomplished Yogis could if they so choose. But for the most part, it was movements that seemed small but with big effects. One of the asanas they both liked the most was shava asana. She had to be as still as a lifeless body but without the negative connotations. She had to lie down on her back on a mat or a thick carpet. The body, including the mind, had to be still, relaxed, part by part, starting with the toe –'Move your big toe up and down and relax it. Relax the rest of your foot. Relax your ankles, relax your knees, relax your thighs…' When it was over and she lay in that state for 10 minutes, she felt rested in a way different from sleep.

Rajiv imagined every part of her beautiful self, relaxing as he gave directions, and it filled him with ecstasy. He recited the *Devi Kavach* to her, explaining how it visualised every part of her body being protected by Durga.

The summer sky was beautiful. It had a typical light pastel blue colour. Catherine felt that she was floating in it. Everything was touched with magic. It was almost unreal. One felt like reaching out to touch it. The light tree trunks were bathed in sunlight, the tips of the leaves were made with sparkling gold.

Sometimes they drove through Golf Links. There were signs on the internal roundabouts:

> 'Welcome to Golf Links
> Please drive carefully
> We love our children.'

The row houses all along the large rectangular gardens seemed enchanted, some of the corner ones mysterious and inviting.

At other times they took the long and winding Ratendone Road, later called Amrita SherGill Marg after the Indo-Hungarian painter who had been so creative in her short life. One couldn't tell where the road was going, it seemed to be leading beyond the horizon. It had unexpected curves along which were pleasant looking bungalows of different types.

When they took this road back towards her house, it would sometimes take them to the corner shop in Jor Bagh market. It had a foreign air about it. It would be full of foreign edible items, especially foreign chocolates as well as foreign magazines with sexy, nubile women on the covers, at a time when these things were hard to get in India. They would go there and have a Mars or at least a Kwality choc-bar if Rajiv didn't want to splurge on a foreign item.

Rajiv put a flute recital on the turn table. The music was evocative. He managed to communicate some of what it made him feel, of *Siddhartha* by Hermann Hesse and of the vast Indian plains, of a youth playing the flute far away in the distance, in the moonlight. Of Krishna and his magic flute at night and the enchantment it spread on the Gopis and everywhere.

It wasn't just one thing. It was a whole host of factors that made India the centre of gravity in the late '60s. It wasn't just Ravi Shankar, Maharishi Mahesh Yogi, the Beach Boys, Mia Farrow, Donovan, The Beatles, not just their visit to Rishikesh, the songs that they got inspiration for but their interest in Indian classical music. It was the Hare Krishna movement dancing on the main streets of major cities of the West, it was Yoga and many different forms of meditation, colourful Indian textiles and flowing Indian kurtas and saris which went well with the psychedelia of the time. It was coming into contact with other sitarists, Flute players of Indian classical music. It was the commonplace way in which pot was used. It was the attitude to being driven about money that fitted well with the values of the counterculture. It was Timothy Leary and Bob Dylan. It was countless young backpackers coming on their spiritual quests to find themselves, amongst them many a famous name. It was a rite of passage. Above all, it was Indian philosophy, its Vedanta and Upanishads, its abstractions and quest for truth. The streets of Delhi and Bombay—entry points into India and in the case of the former, the gateway to the mystical Himalayas, were flooded with beautiful young people, as in the song.

Catherine had won Rajiv's respect from her sensitivity to people, to situations, to different values, cultures, ways of doing and looking at things.

Catherine adored America and its idealism. McCarthyism

was a scourge of the past decade. LBJ had taken watershed steps in civil rights. It was fun to belong to a superpower—the no 1. Always open to ideas, to innovation. 'Whoopee!' she said to Rajiv. She was lucky to belong to such a country. Springsteen had not yet sung 'Born in the USA!'

She found that Rajiv too shared her idealistic image of America. He thought there was no better place on earth and not just because of the beautiful folk, rock, pop music, Hollywood films, the comics he had so loved, Walter Lantz, Hanna-Barbera, Margie's and Walt Disney, to name just some coming out of America. Then there were the Westerns like Zane Grey portraying an idyllic landscape with romance so beautiful that it made his heart yearn, and comics like Gunsmoke, Bonanza, Cheyenne, Wells Fargo, Lone Ranger and the Maverick Brothers. When he talked about America, a faraway look filled his eyes. He described a place which had an azure blue sky with fleecy white clouds scattered at random. It was called El Paso, not that either of them had been there. Or golden, pastoral landscapes, in the afternoon, next to a small, lovely pond with sunlit trees encircling it, like on the cover of a Billy Vaughn album or as evoked by the music of 'A Summer Place'.

Rajiv discovered to his pleasure that Catherine played a mean hand of tennis, with a very fast serve and excellent baseline strokes. She looked most fetching in her white tennis T-shirt and shorts. The American expat community had a bowling place. She took him there. He got a kiss the first time he downed all ten skittles. She teamed up with him in a croquet game, AFS versus the American School. They did well together. He got a high from her approbation. In India there was this obscure game of cricket, played by a dozen countries which she'd heard about and which was visible everywhere. She loved dancing, not just the faster ones, which Rock music seemed tailor made for, but also dances like the Waltz, which she could do skilfully. This was one more point of commonality with Rajiv.

Rajiv had found good quality charas in Delhi; it was easy and cheap, especially in the University area and he and Catherine smoked thin rolls of it, without any tobacco, while listening to new music. He also found some in his own garden.

There would be the sweet smell of marijuana at some of the Indian classical music concerts he took her to. He would be dressed in starched white kurta pyjama, as would she; she looked stunning in it. It seemed made to measure for her.

Some early evenings, with the sun setting, a bunch of kids sat in a circle, took slow deliberate puffs and passed the joint to each other after each drag. Once there was just the two of them. She stroked the hair away from his forehead.

Rajiv took her to lovely marble floored movie halls like Plaza, Rivoli, Odeon, Regal to watch movies in dark matinee shows on blazing afternoons.

'Have you read *Return to Peyton Place*?'

'Wicked,' she giggled with a glint in her eye. Was she pulling his leg?

'I think I'm falling for you,' he said.

'I be silly,' she said with the faintest trace of a smile. She looked utterly desirable.

Catherine kissed him and smiled, snapping her fingers.

'Has the kiss sent you somewhere or brought you back from somewhere?'

Catherine was becoming more and more important and he was falling headlong in love with her.

They talked about *The Picture of Dorian Grey* one day as they drove in the Fiat towards Jor Bagh. She listened with rapt attention. She was wearing an Irish green sweater. It brought out her complexion. He kissed her upturned face at a bend in the road where it seemed to turn towards nowhere. The Fiat 1100 had such terrific pick-up. Out of the cars available then, it was by far the best. It was sturdy and as he changed gears and revved on the wide empty avenues and roads of New Delhi, making them feel like they were in the Grand Prix.

'Where did that come in?' she smiled.

'It was too inviting,' he said laughing, 'you were listening so earnestly.'

'How else should I have listened?'

'Always with such innocence.'

Aparna hosted another get together for the AFS crowd and invited some friends. The Stones sang:

'It's so hard just to have one Girl
When there's a million in the world'

Rajiv sang along with a jaunty, rakish air. 'This is the swinging sixties.'

'Absolutely,' she said. Just then a guy, Gaurav, cut in. Rajiv saw that he was extremely handsome. Rajiv waited for one song to be over. Maybe Gaurav would bow out. He didn't. Rajiv gritted his teeth and waited for the second song to be over before reclaiming Catherine.

He talked about whatever he was reading, whatever he was thinking. She was only one year younger but he felt intellectually advanced and wanted to share with her from his elevated vantage point.

They read some plays out to each other. Rajiv tried out his voice projection and read with perfect enunciation, like in College auditions for the Shakespeare Society or other Thespian endeavours. This was an art to be honed and cultivated.

One evening they watched Louis Bunuel. Some of the scenes were so absurd that Rajiv was in splits. Catherine caught his infectious laughter and neither of them could stop laughing.

Long into the night, after the movie was over, their laughter kept getting triggered over the smallest things. Neither could stop.

They started doing things every day. This segued into lunch and dinner. Time became timeless. There was an unexpected intensity to things. An Exchange visit and this? He started picking her up at 9 a.m. and drive her around the wide avenues of Akbar Road, PrithviRaj and Tughlaq roads, Shanti Path and the narrow deserted by lanes next to beautiful embassies like those of Sweden and Switzerland. Sometimes she would meet him in front of the Post Office in Nizamuddin. She chose it for no reason at all. Aparna would drop her there or she would walk, the heat at that time of the day didn't bother her. She'd wear a bright dress. It would go well with her and the bright light would highlight everything—the buildings, the trees, her blonde hair. She would be standing next to the red post box as he'd drive up.

He would bring her home for a glass of freshly squeezed fruit juice and put on some music. She loved that. He would put on Schumann or Mozart, Tchaikovsky or Beethoven's 'Pastoral Symphony'. They both loved 'Swan Lake' and 'Pictures at an Exhibition' and Chopin's 'Nocturnes' and 'Piano concertos'. They would hear Bach and imagine themselves running naked in the forest.

Time stretched like a rubber band. They heard 'Claire de Lune' and other compositions of Debussy, of Mendelssohn and saw the moistness forming at the corner of her eyes. It had only been a few days. But what moments can do.

Other moments, the record player would play 'I've got love going for me, Colour my World', lovely songs of Petula Clark and 'No Salt on Her Tail, Dedicated to the One I Love' or other beautiful melodies of The Mamas & The Papas. There would always be Dusty Springfield. Once, when she was leaving, the song that came on was 'The minute you're gone'.

'Rajiv...' she started.

'What?'

'Nothing...' she trailed off.

'Liar,' he said, looking into her eyes.

She yawned and stretched suddenly. He put his arms around her, before she could put them down.

They kissed simultaneously. It was hard to say who had kissed whom first. They kept their mouths closed, found themselves exchanging many rapid kisses.

Gradually, their kisses lengthened. Enormous tension seemed to be getting released from both.

They kissed more urgently. Their mouths started opening more. Neither wanted it to be over. Rajiv could think of nothing else. He sensed she felt the same.

They sat on the sofa and kissed. They could not stop. Only interrupted when the Long Playing Record had to be changed, or the eight 45 Singles the Record changer could take ran out. They heard 'All you need is Love', 'Don't go out into the rain, sugar', 'Please don't go' as the 45s made their own juke box.

Catherine and Rajiv sat side by side, right next to each other and look at the stunning pictures in *Seventeen*, *Life* magazine. Of landscapes, important events, pretty girls wearing mini-skirts and maxis, of girls with straw coloured hair flying in the wind in the prairies. The long afternoons shone brightly, punctuated only by the lulling sound of afternoon birds. The leaves formed ever-changing patterns on the walls. They seemed made to measure for Simon and Garfunkel's 'Patterns'.

Rajiv thought her perfect but had enough maturity to know that this wouldn't be the case. Maybe it was his idealism, his youth, his projections. He subconsciously put her on a pedestal. Other than pure long kisses, which he wished would never end, the relationship hadn't been very physical.

He took her to a morning show of *Doctor Zhivago*. They had both seen it but they were swept away by the romance of it.

Rajiv would pick her up as soon as her schedule would allow and drop her home as late as possible. It was working its way towards full moon and the bright moonlit night would hide the hour, the clock showing whatever impossible time.

Rajiv's parents and siblings too saw the intense look on his face, the far-away look in his eyes. Could things move so fast and what would they mean when she was gone? But Catherine and Rajiv devoured every minute of the present and nothing else mattered.

Ringo sang, 'Would you believe in a love at first sight? Yes I'm certain that it happens all the time... What would you do if I turned out the lights? I can't tell you but I know it's mine ...'

Catherine bought him an Iris Murdoch. On it she wrote:

> 'I awoke from dreams of thee
> In the first sweet sleep of night
> When the moon was shining low
> And the stars were shining bright.'

And in small letters—'a variation on Shelley'

She liked the way Rajiv looked, his well-defined and well-proportioned features, the softness in his face, his brown eyes, his pale brown almost golden complexion, so attractively different. Rajiv's chest, his inner wrists had an even more appealing hue, indefinable in the nomenclature of tonality.

For Catherine, it was a lot of learning. Sometimes, Rajiv took her out for an Indian meal. She tried to eat a Tandoori Chicken cooked red with lemon on the side with a knife and fork. It wasn't the same as eating Chicken a la Kiev with implements. The tandoori chicken pieces lent themselves best to being picked up and bitten into. That was why it was obligatory before Indian meals to wash hands. The implements for some things were the fingertips of the right hand. Only one hand was to be used. Tandoori roti was even more difficult with a knife and fork. Once Catherine got into it, she commented on how sensuous it was and how much she preferred it for certain items.

A silver bowl appeared at the end of the meal with a delicate slice of lemon floating in it.

'What is this, Rajiv? Is this to digest the meal?'

'Touch it, Catherine. The water is warm, slightly more than tepid. This is a finger bowl for cleaning your fingers after certain dishes.'

'The other day at the same place, the waiter took away your plate even though there was food still on it. How did he know you had finished?'

'In America you must be doing it differently. I had placed my knife and fork together vertically at right angles to the plate... It's English, I imagine. That was a sign I had finished.'

Rajiv would drive her from Nizamuddin and take Lodhi Road going past Tibet House, the sun would light up his face with a heavenly orange light, particularly in the evenings. They were on the road to nowhere, just going for a drive in the cool moisture laden breeze wherever the fancy took them, her blonde hair flying in the wind. She would smile and they would talk or sing a song together or put on something on the car cassette like 'Snoopy and the Red Baron' or something else and drive down the beautiful, wide, tree lined boulevards and avenues. He put a hand on her knee and withdrew it if there was a higher vehicle like a truck passing from the left.

They would turn on to the unforgettable road past Golf Links with the club on one side and trees next to the houses and in the middle aisle. The houses along the road were large and varied. He wondered about the people who lived in them. There was one called 'Nora's Villa', with light blue walls. It seemed like a piece of Blueberry pie. There were the crescents. There was the Embassy of Poland in the corner of one such. There was the Mongolian Embassy, with a dark blue painted emblem on the gate. Once they saw a Mongolian boy leaning out of the second floor window, brushing his already very white teeth. They highlighted his features. Rajiv imagined deeply evocative songs typical of the Orient coming from far away.

They went to some of the lovely book shops in Khan Market, smelling of books. There were so many appealing looking new books with enticing covers. Even the comics and their annuals looked like they had to be bought. They were holding hands. It was raining outside. Everything had a faraway feel.

Rajiv took her to many of the monuments dotted all over Delhi and they kissed in the shelter of the arches and secret nooks. She felt herself transported to mediaeval times, the tombs and the gardens still felt like that.

As she got more familiar with them, they both got the same idea spontaneously and they slipped into Lodi Gardens once late at night. The shapes of individual edifices punctuated by the vast open spaces in between. Those days were not so paranoiac. It was easy to do that. There were many gaps in the boundary walls, which were not high in any case. When they woke up, it was already early morning. No one had disturbed them. There was dew on the grass and the starlight was on their faces. They were aware of a sense of something happening.

Friends of Rajiv and Catherine knew them to be very romantic, who felt deeply. They recognised this in each other pretty soon. It takes one to know one.

Rajiv thought of her heavenly smile. He looked out of the window at the large moon, so near, tossed and turned, got up and walked in the soft, scented night outside. He could think of nothing or no one else. He drove to Catherine's house, at least she was still in India. What was she doing? Was she feeling any of this? She must have heard a sound outside the window or sensed his presence. She opened the window, a pale figure framed against the moonlight and put her long thin arms, sticking out of her sky-blue nightie, around his neck.

They danced wildly in The Cellar many nights, lost themselves in the lovely music, the vibrations. There was a sense of bonhomie and camaraderie with visiting flower people, for whom Delhi and India were a pilgrimage.

There was no closing hour for the discotheques. Catherine and Rajiv would lose track of time and dance till 1 or 2 a.m. Tireless. Driven by the energy of all the fellow dancers. They would only get aware of the time when driving home.

The scented evenings of the summer, full of character and lengthening shadows, had a bluish tinge to them. The night would come filled with the ubiquitous fragrance of summer flowers and the Mughal monuments silhouetted against the unbelievably silvery moonlight.

He bought white night jasmine moistened in water to preserve the freshness from the sellers at India Gate to take home with her when she parted. They were sleepless. It didn't seem to affect them the next morning. A dance party would wind up on Tughlaq Road or Kushak Road or Vasant Vihar. It would already be 3 a.m. The music would still be in their heads. There would be a late night feel to the city. Rajiv would drive her to the 24-hour coffee shop. It was always pleasant, always welcoming, always open. They would order Cold Coffee sometimes with ice cream or Rajiv would ask for extra liquid sugar which would come in a small silver jug. He had not yet discovered that this was an Indian thing and if one ordered cold coffee in America, one would get iced black coffee. The cold coffee had lots of milk with the taste and aroma of coffee. Sometimes they would order a soup or a samosa to go with it. All the dancing would make them hungry and these dance parties had dinner as the last thing on everyone's mind. The music, the dancing, the beautiful, graceful sarees were it. Sometimes there would be the sweet smell of Pot, for those who chose to light up while escorting their partner around with one arm. The seating arrangement next to the large oblong marble tables was so comfortable, the ambience so elegant, the lighting so pleasing that they would linger. Above all, it was each other's company. They didn't run out of things to say.

His parents worried. There were no cell phones. No way of knowing whether Rajiv was alright. Rajiv didn't want to worry them. But he couldn't give up these timeless, unforgettable nights.

Some nights he resorted to putting bolsters in the shape of his sleeping form under the cover. He became an expert at that. In the darkened room, he could have fooled himself. It had to be that good.

Rajiv was a dependent member of the Delhi Gymkhana Club, in the days when it was still sophisticated. Dances were in the Central Hall and people Fox Trotted, Jived, Cha Chaed and Waltzed skilfully. He took her dancing there and they would get lost in it and the music. He marvelled at her long limbs and how she moved them.

The talk here too was similar to the one in College—articles read in *Encounter* or the plays of Giradoux and Genet, the books of Scott Fitzgerald and Nathaniel Hawthorne.

The lawn between the main Club building and the covered pool was a vast expanse of green, peopled by tall trees to one side instead of food stalls and tables. The covered Pool was virtually deserted in the evening, providing plenty of opportunity to Rajiv and Catherine to play in the pool, be splashed by each other and to hang at either end and talk.

They sat in the colonnaded verandah of one of his close friends in a bungalow typical of Lutyens Delhi and sipped gin and lime. Gin didn't give one a headache, felt light and refreshing and was not only colourless but odourless too. He told her about how in the vast tea estates gin and tonic was the drink of choice. It gave protection against mosquitoes and somehow seemed appropriate to the surroundings. For Coffee drinking Catherine it was another world. He told her about the many varieties of teas and the differences in tea plucking. He took her to Aap ki pasand in Darya Ganj, where she could sample infinite flavours of tea before buying if she wanted.

They listened to Sinatra's inimitable music—and Elvis singing 'Summer Kisses, Winter Tears' or 'Sound Advice', which sprang out of the unique terroir of America. Like its own wine. At other times it was the typical virtuosity of American music like Gershwin's 'A Rhapsody in Blue' or Duke Ellington.

'Sitar music too is like Jazz,' he told her when they listened to Ravi Shankar or other masters. It has a lot of improvisation like Jazz does. It can be incredibly complex and difficult to play. It is very mathematical but in a different way.

Catherine spent the minimum possible time on the field report she had to give at the end of the trip. (What would she write? That she met this guy at the beginning of her trip and it took up her whole time?) But Catherine was observant and sensitive. And a fast worker. An informative and useful report was a work in progress. There was not much other structure to comply with. Her host family took their cue from Aparna and were indulgent. They saw that she looked radiant and gave up on seeing much of her.

The time together stretched and felt rich enough for a lifetime. Catherine and Rajiv felt the specialness of every moment. To capture the *fugace*. To live in it. To be fully aware of it. To seize it. They couldn't live it any better.

Catherine had liked Ashoka and they decided to go another day. 'C'mon, race you,' she said. Rajiv was reluctant. He didn't feel like it.

'Oh, c'mon,' she urged. Rajiv put his head down and swam free style. Rajiv's style looked good, but she won, even though she did breast strokes. Did she take a bigger push from the wall?

'No fair, doing free style,' she said.

'But I automatically did that, I thought you would too.'

'Sore winner,' he added with a grin. His leg accidentally brushed against hers and he felt electricity. She pushed his head under water and he flailed his arms about and pretended to be drowning.

The rainy season had set in and the sky suddenly darkened even though it was afternoon. 'Darkness at noon,' she said. Rajiv told her he loved swimming in the rain. It was never too cold and there was a sense of adventure swimming in the pool with it pouring buckets from above. As soon as your head popped out of the water you got totally drenched with water from the heavens. And it was so dark and dramatic, it was hard to believe the clock.

He chased her in the sudden darkness as she swam towards the horizon, sheets of water making it seem that. Someone had upturned a corresponding swimming pool in the heavens. No matter how stormy there was the safety of knowing this was a pool and not the sea with its inhuman waves.

After the rain the sky was a startling blue, everything was washed, there was no summer dust in the air, the light was golden and clear and the leaves of the trees and bushes a very different chlorophyll green.

The next evening, at the crossing leading from Janpath to Connaught Place while stopped at the red light, Rajiv looked at her from the steering wheel and said, 'The trouble with you is…'

She listened in silence but he could see she was surprised and felt put down. That hadn't been his intention, though he felt what he said was true. She replied by the time they crossed the light. She was cross. The atmosphere in the car was strained.

He stopped the car near Regal cinema. There was a softy machine there. He hopped out and bought two strawberry softies. They looked tempting but she shook her head.

There was a morning show of *How to Steal a Million* with Peter O' Toole at Odeon, he remembered. On an impulse he proposed they see that. They had both seen it but it was such a lovely movie. She was tempted. In the movie after half an hour, he slid his hand into hers. She accepted it. Pax.

Like his friends, Rajiv had come across an absurdity when going through the American admission process. TOEFL—ridiculous, Indians are English speaking. English is an Indian language too. But they had to do it. The application process was inflexible. Catherine also saw how ridiculous it was. Indians were invariably in the very highest percentiles. If Americans took it, they would score no higher. Sometimes lower. It was a hoop that had to be jumped though.

'Why don't they make Australians take it? Had part of it been oral, nobody would have understood their accent. Why us? Surely they could have made an exception of those who went to English medium schools in India and there were so many of them.'

All the people he knew, all his friends from other schools

too were English speaking, as were the courts and a large section of the press. Was this American ignorance about the rest of the world?

The other odd thing he noticed was that though Catherine and he were only a year and a half apart, he would go to the Senior Year, whereas Catherine would only be a Freshman. Americans graduated from High School when they were 18.

2

Catherine talked about her plans. Her friends and classmates were mostly going to one of the Seven Sisters. That was her family tradition too. She had made campus visits to all the places she was considering, with her parents, the previous year.

'Have you only considered Liberal Arts, Humanities, Catherine?'

'Odd that you ask that, Rajiv, I do actually have an interest in Business. I have grown up in a business environment.'

'Me too,' interrupted Rajiv.

'So, I have considered doing an MBA but let me finish Undergrad first and then I'll see. There are very few girls in an MBA class still, though it'll probably change with time. May be 4 out of 50. And there are still some whose thoughts of "What is a nice girl like you doing in a business school" will be pretty evident.'

She hadn't wanted to apply to too many places. Catherine, before coming on the field trip, had found the voluminous application process to universities tedious and cumbersome, some of the details pernickety. It was a welcome relief not being burdened with this when she landed in India.

She would have had to get her teachers to send that many more referrals. And one needed the mental space to think of so many places. One of the places she had thought of was Vassar. It was going co-ed in 1969. A huge step. That would take some of the pressure off for interaction with boys, was the thinking. Of course, she would have had more opportunities to meet young men there. Yale had offered merger/affiliation to its unofficial sister college, a proposal to move Vassar to New Haven, 75 miles, almost two hours away. Vassar had a large (1000 acres) beautiful campus, elegant architecture of the college with its classical styles, Vassar Lake and lots of scope for walking, contemplation, especially in the fall. It had quads and Halls of residence with a room for each student. But it was in Poughkeepsie, which rivalled only New Haven in being a totally unremarkable place except for the University. So, throughout the week there was nothing but the cloistered existence of Vassar campus.

Yale was already the brother college of Vassar or more appropriately the boyfriend college. Vassar turned down Yale's offer of merging. The local press called it—'The marriage that never was.'

Acceptance in a very good school was no indicator of acceptance in another, even if one had got in to a place where the acceptance rate was lower. Catherine was very pleased when she did get an admission letter.

She had applied to Smith in Northampton, Massachusetts but she had not got admission. One could hardly get in everywhere, she added, and there were a lot of good candidates applying to many places. They had to choose and select.

Catherine had made enquiries from her network, cousins of friends, extended family about Wellesley. Wellesley in Massachusetts was 17 miles, about half an hour to Boston. There was an unofficial close connection with MIT. It was part of the Greater Boston area, in fact. So, her big city needs could be fulfilled over weekends. The 500-acre campus was considered a dream campus. Vast majority of students found dorm quality great.

Freshmen had to live on campus. By all accounts, social life was not good. There were some decent house parties but they were on weekends only. [15]

The fateful admission letter failed to turn up.

She had also got admission at Mount Holyoke, in Massachusetts. It was 1 ½ hours, 90 miles to Boston from South Hadley. NY was 2 hours and 40 minutes—155 miles.

Catherine managed to talk to some recently graduated alums of Mount Holyoke, daughters of parents' friends and acquaintances. The core of the College was undergrad at Mount Holyoke. She wanted to go to a place where she could continue Grad work in the same place. MA existed, consisting of Seminars, a thesis, but it was on the periphery. That was not what the college was all about.

Rajiv told her it was the same in Delhi University. You begin to feel what are you doing there, if you are still there. Colleges no longer have separate lectures. They are all in the University, combined with other colleges. Its heart was in the three undergrad years that flew away like magic and in the intimate and special life of each college.

Mount Holyoke had Mixers, mostly with Amherst but sometimes with Harvard and other colleges in the area. These Mixers were looked forward to, to relieve the tedium, to have contact with boys, who, like in all such circumstances, became strange creatures. They were few and far between. Catherine had also heard how desperate the young women would become. The mass exodus over weekends was too obvious to be denied. But that was common to all the Seven Sisters.

Over the weekend someone who didn't have plans would be worse than a wallflower. Friday afternoon they would be falling down the stairs to catch the Greyhound bus to wherever the Mixer had been organised by some of the girls. And there in the dances they would stand around until someone asked them to dance. The boys would have their pick.

There were no official arrangements for overnight stay. It was unthinkable to come back before Sunday. They would have to crash with other girls or stay over with one of the boys who had picked them up.

The Greyhound bus would be functional at best, nowhere near the romance of the trains that had built America in the previous century. The Greyhound took 2 ½ hours to NY and Boston was 2 hours.

The places to stay over functional, Catherine was told. The whole experience was not memorable, unless, of course, you were one of the lucky few who met someone charming and sophisticated.

And yet a few weekends later, there one would be hurrying not to miss the bus, having sworn to oneself not to go again unless there was something special.

Marriage prospects were not spoken about overtly, Catherine had heard, but some girls did hope to find a rich husband. Some would get married immediately after graduation irrespective of these Mixers.

International students were housed in (Emily) Dickenson House, named after their famous alum. Some Americans could also find place there. There were separate rooms with shared bathrooms. These halls were in a cluster—all together.

In the Undergrad dorm one had breakfast, lunch and dinner. Each dorm was called a Hall. Each hall of residence had a kitchen and dining room. Some of the less well-off girls supplemented their income by waitressing.

These Halls were absolutely mysterious for boys. They never entered any.

South Audley—the place had nothing else. One went to

Stores and Record for books and music and bought Prints in Poster shops to decorate one's room.

Papers had to be submitted for tutorials. There was a lot of reading material for each. The curriculum would be highly structured—there would be no time left unplanned. 'That would appeal to me,' said Rajiv.

'Well, it did, me too—that part,' agreed Catherine.

'There will be lectures and Professors often hold the Seminars at their places. That is cosy and informal, girls told me.'

So that was two out of the four Seven Sisters she had applied to.

The education would be excellent, the prestige and how it would look in her CV immeasurable. But the bottom line was how she wanted to spend four precious years at this crucial point of her life. More than other things it was the quality of her time. She was confident of her future in conventional terms.

Having grown up in New York, could she imagine such a sheltered existence? In places like the Seven Sisters, she had heard about the weekend pressure and desperation that built up.

The outlier from the point of view of her Upper East Side family she had daringly applied to was UC Berkeley. It would be a liberal, emancipated place. It was the centre of so much change, new ideas. For a city person like her, it was next door to San Francisco, with all its offerings. A degree from there would be no less valued. Its academic credentials, the quality of its professors, was excellent. It was a Continent away; it would be a big change.

The job market in upper crust New York would be far better with the Ivy League than radical Berkeley. What did she really want? What would make her happier? The freedom of Berkeley or the training imparted by the tested and tried?

She discussed with Rajiv about how torn she had been

between her long family tradition from both sides, of Ivy League or Seven Sisters and the counterpoint of Berkeley. Confined existence there, to freedom of California. There was considerable parental pressure, not to mention larger family, to stay with prestige. It was the safer thing to do, with many advantages. She would be better trained if she wanted to enter the world of Business. Finally, she sent her acceptance of Admission to Mount Holyoke by the due date in May, before leaving for India. Reluctantly, she dropped Vassar, there was not much to choose from between the two. At the last minute she also sent it to UC Berkeley. 'Walk on the Wild Side,' she said to herself. She could get her money back from Holyoke without withdrawn mentioned on the transcript, if she withdrew by a date in July, well before term started. That would be while she was still in India. UC Berkeley, being a state University, had minimal cost for her in any case.

She had thought a lot about it, she told him. In the final analysis it had been a tough decision. But there were deadlines. She had to send in her acceptance before her trip to India.

Her parents were not too happy about it. Apart from other things, it would be hard to lose their daughter. Have her living so far away. But they believed in Catherine taking her own decisions about how she lived her life. And she still might end up choosing Mount Holyoke.

Mount Holyoke had easy payment plans in five instalments. The first instalment was not immediately after acceptance but well into the summer. Even after admission, the withdrawal with full refund plan was extremely liberal. There were dates set well in advance for 100 per cent refund without anything/ WDR appearing on the transcript. Even after that it was possible with a reducing percentage of refunds. Nothing could be more open minded and flexible.

Before her trip to India, Mount Holyoke had been the front runner. Rajiv had tilted the balance. If this was the effect of losing her head, so be it.

'Rajiv, I'm going to withdraw from Mount Holyoke and go to Berkeley.'

'Mount Holyoke couldn't be more prestigious—it is in the East. Its Gestalt is Class, it is upper class or upper middle class by and large. Berkeley has a high academic standard but its connotations are completely different. In the job market, in professional development, they are two different worlds. There is no comparison.

'The West Coast is another world. It is a continent away. The flying time is almost the same as going from India to Europe. The political culture is much more Left, which is great but it is a big change. It's called the People's Republic of Berkeley,' Rajiv agreed as both laughed.

'As I live through these times it is becoming clearer and clearer that I love the Sixties and all that is a part of it. This is part of my self-realisation and what better place than India for that. Berkeley/San Francisco is the apogee of that. I will really experience it there. Education is equally about that. Most of all, that's where you've got admission, Rajiv. I'm not going to be separated from you, more than I can help it.'

The Seven Sisters would be part of the Roads not taken. They would have to survive without each other till Rajiv could come over.

3

'I *will* come, Catherine. I will do my damnedest, and there is no reason why I won't succeed. I never imagined or anticipated that that one evening could have led to this. Not in the least to say I don't want more, a lifetime with you. But this has already given me that much. This was our summer, Catherine, our holidays. It's turned out to be a beautiful summer love, though that has transient connotations and that's not what I'm referring to. I'm just referring to the magic of this summer with all the intensity that an Indian summer has.'

'Me too,' she said softly. 'I will follow you, Rajiv, to the ends of the earth. If you can't come, I will come here. I will live where you live.'

'You are highly intelligent and creative Catherine. It is evident to anyone who gets to know you. You have to be independent. Your active mind has to be occupied. We will have to find something meaningful for you here in that case.'

'We'll cross that bridge when we come to it, Rajiv. Where there is will there is a way, to use a cliché. For the time being, we both have to finish our studies and we are both aiming to do that in America. Meantime, we have had this and nothing can take this unforgettable summer away from us,' she agreed.

'It has been an eternity. There are so many ways of measuring time. India produces strong reactions in foreigners. They either love it or hate it. It's an intense experience. Just the colour you come across, for example. I'm yet to come across a middle way reaction. I'm thankful you are in the former category.'

One evening, as the shadows lengthened and the stars began to appear, Rajiv sang, 'If I give my heart to you, do you promise to be true.'

Catherine smiled. He could have died. Heartbreaker.

Rajiv wrote in his diary—With Catherine...a pure sort of love that was leading to desire... With Ayesha, desire that had led to love... Different trajectories.

Their kisses were long and Time lost its dimension. It would be enchantment. There was the feeling, the awareness, at each moment that this was the love of their lives. During the kiss, Chopin or Beethoven's 'Fifth' would be on or 'Theme from A Summer Place'. There was no contact deeper than this.

Rajiv thought that their dreams were built on a lot of hope but there was a lot of uncertainty inherent in the situation. Not the least of it was resources to fund his education. And dollars translated into many more rupees. This was not based on Purchasing Power parity but on an exchange rate decided by the government. He had got admission but that was only the half of it. Catherine was going back to her own country, somewhere she had grown up, was comfortable with, in the final analysis, no matter how much she had taken to India. Sometimes, America seemed like a dream. Would he be able to realise it, actually land there?

Was he doomed to these unbearable partings? A déjà vu? Soon, it'll be over. And I'll be gone. That summer had been a life time. If they got nothing more, would it suffice? A *Roman Holiday* kind of parting?

Nizamuddin is one of the nicest colonies, particularly Nizamuddin East with its pleasantly designed houses, melange of Muslim and Hindu cultures, proximity not just to Humayun's Tomb but to other Mughal ruins with large parks surrounding them. They had gone to many dance parties there. It was here on a small balcony one charmed afternoon with everything still and quiet that they had kissed and he had said softly, 'I love you,' and was surprised and delighted to hear a whispered, almost inaudible, 'Me too.'

The next day he took her to some of the Jewellers in Connaught Place. She selected a ring. It was simple and elegant. The gold had such a pleasing hue and the diamond sparkled. 'We are engaged as of now,' he said. She just looked fetching. Neither of them was as yet 21, but they were sure. Life was inconceivable without the other. The Power of Love.

'Breakfast at Tiffany's.'

The ardour felt could not remain at the level of kissing. There was this all-consuming desire to be one, to assuage the emotional ache.

They went to the Air India office next door to reconfirm Catherine's ticket reservation. Rajiv also made enquiries about his own ticket. He was to follow her as soon as possible. The young man behind the counter gave them good vibrations.

Many they came into contact with sensed the romance and rejoiced in it. There was something contagious about it and Rajiv thought that it must be true that 'All the world loves a lover'. When they were thrown into that insane state, strange ladies smiled at them. It would have been the same in Paris or Berkeley.

Catherine kept looking at Rajiv, deep into his eyes, from the adjoining counter seat, asking him with her eyes and saying softly now and then, 'You will? Tonight?' He couldn't have been more flattered or pleased. He loved her so.

Chez Rajiv, their mouths were back together in a tempestuous kiss, which seemed to draw everything out of them. Both were overcome. Revelled in it. It was Ravel. Swam and sank in it. The longing led to further creativity. The experimentation in their kissing was spontaneous. Sometimes the clinch was broken for that reason. There was the old and the new. It temporarily assuaged the ache within.

Their clothes came off. They weren't even aware of it happening. All that mattered was that they continue to kiss. Rajiv felt the coolness of her breasts next to his. He savoured her mouth. She kissed him in a way that made him dizzy. He felt her loosening his belt and unzipping his trousers. She pulled down his trousers and then his underwear. He was rock solid. There no longer was the underwear holding him down, restraining him. She pulled down her own maxi-like Tartan dress. It suited her so. Finally, there was only the pantie. Their kiss was extremely passionate now. He pulled it off. He glided inside as smooth as butter. It was completely automatic at that stage. Their attention was still on their kiss and their mouths rivetted together, not on the love making taking place below.

Once they went beyond kissing, it's as if a dam was unleashed. Overwhelming love. The physical aspect was just a manifestation of it. There was the desire to be one, one being, to be united. There was the pent-up ache of it, the pain of it, the yearning.

They continued to hold each other and to look in each other's eyes, the more passionate kisses gave way to much gentler kisses, the emotional closeness was not lost. They were still one in mind and spirit. They must have dozed off for a while. The night was almost over. There was the exhilarating exhaustion of being loved. 'I'll be loving you Eternally'.

The day of departure inevitably came. It was bound to happen. All the AFS students and their host families came to the airport. Rajiv saw two of the girls crying, their faces were red. 'Why are they crying? Won't they ever come back again? Is it so difficult?' he wondered. Everyone, including the

AFS coordinators, went right up to the wire fence just before the tarmac. The world was still innocent then. Man had not perpetrated hijacking on man yet.

Catherine looked at him long on the final day at the airport. Rajiv went beyond the fence separating the tarmac from the area where everyone was standing. No one stopped him as Catherine walked towards the plane. It was a typical monsoon day. Windy. She turned back to look at him at the foot of the stairs leading up to the plane and at the top. Her look conveyed everything. Rajiv stood there, a lean, very young, solitary figure, looking at the horizon as the wind blew his raincoat and hair. The air was moisture laden and the rain a little while ago had brought up the smell of the earth and the grass. There was the typical hum of the plane receding until it became a dot in the sky. A fermata.

The AFS coordinators gave him an understanding smile as he turned back. He didn't know where to go from here. It was too tame to go back. He stopped at the place of one of his all-night party friends. Rajiv's whole body language conveyed it.

'How are you?' his friend asked him.

'Turbulent.'

4

Not only are all of us interconnected, even supposedly temporary encounters are actually not temporary at all. 'They leave their footprints,' he thought.

Rajiv wrote in his diary—I had finally grown up and my adolescence was over, if that is what it was. It often takes longer than we care to recognise or admit. As long as one enjoys the journey. I had come of age, if that is what it was.

Rajiv wrote her long letters and got lovely letters on blue paper that carried a whiff of her. That alone made everything worth it. It was so her. She sent her photos in some of them. It made him long for her. How had he been so lucky that she had come into his life?

Her thoughts on many things. They were full of news. How she was preparing, what she had done with her family, where all she'd been out with her friends, what was new in her life, what she had read that she liked or didn't think much of, even though it was acclaimed, her reactions to the latest music, the films that had blown her mind, the art exhibitions that she'd been to, the group parties she had attended. She must have danced with someone. Rajiv tried not to feel jealous.

He wrote on onion skin, sometimes on a letter head he got made with his initials. Some of his letters were short with a photo enclosed, others longer. It was the content that mattered. Sometimes he wrote a line on the envelope—something that had caught his imagination, sometimes the paper was tinged with the slightest hint of Old Spice, Aqua Velva, Crest or Monarch.

Once he put a pressed night jasmine in it.

He tried to phone her a few times but it was hopeless. The line would often be bad and crackly. It was limited to a maximum of six minutes, with the operator saying three minutes all too soon. One would have to say 'continue', some of the first three minutes having gone in building up the radio frequency and saying—louder and louder 'can you hear me?'.

Most of the time the operator in India tried once and let it go at that. It was a government service with little accountability.

Rajiv would follow up. They would assure him that they would just do it but nothing would happen. Rajiv would keep waiting for hours, carrying on with his activity with one ear to the phone. He would follow up again, only to get the same meaningless promise. Given the night and day time difference with America, the window of opportunity would pass, with Rajiv left rehearsing all that he wanted to say.

The rare occasions that Rajiv left the phone to go out, they would miraculously try and blame it on him when he checked. Partly, Rajiv learnt to beat the system by booking another call because that would be tried for the first time before the second attempt on the first call.

When he felt desperate, he sent her telegrams. They were expensive and had to be confined to a few words. Their primary means of communication was letters, purportedly by air mail but even that took seven days to America.

Catherine too found it hard to get back to her normal life. She had very strong will power and she was a focussed girl, determined to succeed in ways that she defined. What was she to do? Pine away for Rajiv? Not be true to her love? Not live life to the fullest? What if despite best efforts he didn't make it?

Catherine had seen a different way of living, thinking, being in India. Families lived together, more than one generation—

sometimes three. It worked out well, they had separate rooms. They had their independent lives but were there for each other when needed. Back home in the States, many people left home when they were 18, even more by the time they were 21. She knew going to college was a step in that direction. Many girls would pair off and find their own lodgings, never to return. If it didn't happen in the undergrad years, it was even more likely in the Grad years.

Catherine continued to blossom; she was ravishing. The mirror told her that, as did her parents' friends. She saw it in the eyes of boys she had grown up with. These were the best years of her life. They would be without each other. Each day was equal to ten at some other time and age. There was no help for it.

Rajiv would dream about her, the exquisite enchanted magic time. He would put fragrant flowers, night Jasmine, other summer and monsoon flowers next to his bed.

Parties went on, a continuation of College—most people who had passed out and were going abroad had not yet left for distant shores. Those enrolled in MA in Delhi University kept up dance parties. He too might come across creatures that might blow his mind. They would have to trust each other. But more than trust, it was the ache of being without her, every moment, every day.

The monsoon washed nights were clear and beautiful—the moon between the trees. Other nights would be star studded, making the sky ethereal, a few small fluffy white clouds floating in their own disorder, light after having shed their rain. Rajiv wished Catherine could see this. He wanted to share, also, the dramatic light in the day when it was cloud covered. So dark and it would only be two in the afternoon. Who would believe it? On rainy days the light would change many times, with many tones and hues. She would have to experience it. It would be hard to believe it was on the same day.

He would drive past the tombs and monuments, Chanakyapuri and the Embassy area, and his heart would ache for her. It would have to be shared with her or forsaken. Beauty without her just caused longing.

'I will cut short the summer, Catherine,' he had said to her. 'I will come as soon as I can do all the many Visa and other travel preparations. I know what a vital and charmed time the summer is in the States. I will not let us be without each other.'

'Yes, a lot happens,' she had said, teasing him. 'Who knows who I might meet? My parents may already be planning my coming out parties.'

As soon as Catherine left, Rajiv put his longing for her into preparation or the trip, working 24x7 at it. The formalities in India were endless for going abroad. One had to jump hoop after hoop. One of the Kafkaesque inventions was a device called the P Form. The bureaucracy and the clerks on whom they depended took sadistic pleasure in making one come back the next day or after ten. 'Go to some other miserable office, overladen with dusty, ragged files, for some other clearance first,' he wrote to Catherine. 'It was needless torture, created uncertainty and anxiety.'

He walked the dusty corridors of power armed only with reason and logic. But these seemed non-sequiturs. The attitude was—the answer is no, unless you can convince us otherwise. Or there would be no decision which amounted to the same thing.

'The small thin clerk looked at me sourly. He had power but he could himself not go because of means… That added to his sourness. I had to convince the controller of exchange ultimately,' Rajiv wrote. The permission to leave the country was valid only for 45 days.

He began to wonder if he would actually make it to the shores of America. They had tried to bring certainty into the separation but the doubts would remain till he was actually sitting on the plane.

It was so far, so imponderable, what it was really like. How would he be treated? Had it just been floating along in a distant dream? Would he lose Catherine too, like he had lost Ayesha? Would he in the end just have to be satisfied with these three months?

He remembered the American application process. How long and arduous it had been. Would he even get there in time, leave alone early like he wanted?

Rajiv would have to learn to be self-sufficient. He took time to learn how to sew buttons, iron clothes, cook a few things. His parents had managed everything and there was domestic staff for daily needs.

The struggle for Rajiv was not just with getting the Foreign Exchange. It was also to put the money together. There was the cost of living in America, the air ticket cost. The Dollars, when converted, came to a lot in Rupees. His family was upper-middle class, but this?

Rajiv ran around to get Health certificates—small pox, cholera vaccinations, certified by WHO. That would be the first impediment at the Border in the US after the long flight.

Suddenly, when it really started happening, his parents from being supportive changed, they didn't want to lose their son. He was only 19. He had also become involved with this American girl. Would he come back? Would he stay on there with her? If she did come back, what would life be like with her here? Would she adjust to a joint family living? Would she destroy the family? A way of life?

Rajiv couldn't bare not being with Catherine. He longed

for her, ached for her. He couldn't sleep; he just wanted to go. His father saw his predicament. He was a soft-hearted man. His mother worked through him. She was determined to hold him back as much as possible. His father kept asking him to cry once. Just once. '*Ek bar ro do.*' Rajiv couldn't understand it then. He was torn. If he had cried it would have helped both him and his father but Rajiv was full of a young self-respect. He had to go by 'logic'. He couldn't cry like that. He loved both his parents. He didn't want to make them unhappy but he had to go—it was life and death. In the final analysis he would even have given up Berkeley but he couldn't give up Catherine.

Rajiv's father said that he had a dream—he should wait for three days—Rajiv couldn't go then. Three days later his father would say he had a dream again—Rajiv had to wait; he couldn't go just then. And so, on it went. Rajiv didn't want to displease him. He went along but he felt desperate. Finally, he left on the day the dreaded P Form permission was to expire. He couldn't have waited a day longer.

Clothes for different seasons had to be planned. A lot of shopping. Some gifts for special people he would meet. Unique things, typically Indian. Maybe Cottage Industries would provide them all. Silk scarves were always a hit, some small, beautiful silver statues of Ganesha, Shiva. The Delhi winter got quite cold but Berkeley would be slightly colder. If Catherine went home for Xmas, New York was much colder. He selected his wardrobe carefully. He loved clothes, he loved dressing up for different occasions, looking elegant but he couldn't be too heavy. 'Airlines had thoughts about that,' he wrote to Catherine. Besides, he would have to carry them everywhere. Nor would he have precious foreign exchange to spend on clothes.

At one of her parents' summer parties, one of her aunts said, 'There is a charming young man I want you to meet. I thought of you when I came across him while you were away in India. He is from an old New York family.'

Catherine saw that he was unmistakably handsome. The music was inviting. He asked her to dance. 'Where have you been hiding all my life,' he said. Christopher wanted to dance only with her. He was smooth on the floor. He wanted to see her again the next day. Take her to a discotheque.

Catherine loved dancing. She hesitated. Rajiv wouldn't mind... He was very open minded and prided himself on being a child of the Sixties. He knew how much she enjoyed dancing. It was a fun evening. The music was very pleasant and the psychedelic lights were a turn on. It reminded her of The Cellar. Despite the AC, she was sweating. The sweat of dancing well. Rajiv would have felt accomplished with it.

Christopher asked her again over the weekend. A different discotheque. She enjoyed the dancing and the going out but where was this leading? She told Christopher. She liked him and the dancing was fun but she had a boyfriend and was committed. As long as it was clear, she would be fine with going to discos every now and then. Catherine mentioned the dancing in one of her epistles to Rajiv.

Christopher was not to be so easily dissuaded. He resolved to see where he could get with this girl without questioning her status. He made tempting offers. A glass of wine at one of the trendy Village bars, tickets to an off Broadway show which were difficult to get. She found him amusing and entertaining. He kissed her at an unwary moment. She put a stop to it, though she enjoyed it. She looked sternly at him. He just looked mischievous. This was getting dangerous. It was just as well that she'd be going away to the West Coast soon now.

Finally, it approached Fall and Rajiv winged his way to the wide-open spaces of America—to this mythical land, which he already knew so much about, its music which knew no boundaries, its comics which were ubiquitous—Dell, Superman DC, later Gold Key, its books, its movies. Indians (unlike Americans when going elsewhere) already knew a lot, were well versed in all aspects of American culture. The culture shock is only in seeing it in real. That this dream world, this fantasy world which one only saw on screen, read in books and heard in music, actually exists. It's not some fantasy world out there. You can reach out and touch it, it's hard to believe that it exists for real. Above all, it had Catherine. It would no longer have to be 'Send me the pillow you dream on'.

Catherine thought of their conversation a few days prior to departure. 'There will be the inevitable periods of separation. You are exceedingly attractive. You will come across boys whom you are attracted to. How can that not be. Even after we are officially together, will we stay together? American marriages are breaking up much more than marriages elsewhere and the trend is increasing.'

'Don't be silly, Rajiv. I do love you as you can see and feel. What kind of simplistic, general worry is that?'

After a pause—'How can you generalise about America and me? And won't it be equally devastating for me if it happens?'

'I don't know, in your culture it seems more the norm. You seem to able to survive it more easily.'

'I can't believe what you are sounding like. I thought you were way above such stereotyping. Stop it.'

Then on a softer note,

'Que sera sera. The future's not ours to see
Whatever will be, will be.'

5

Catherine and Rajiv landed in a San Francisco area, where they were both outsiders. The celebrated Summer of love of 1967 had just been over and 1968 was continuing the trend. The flower culture bloomed and blossomed. The major political events taking place at the time, the profusion of beautiful and timeless music profoundly affected both of them.

Everything changed after the restive late '60s. It was a time of unbelievable change, when values were being questioned and there was a cultural revolution (very different from the disastrous one so called in the People's Republic of China, going on at the same time). It seemed the change would endure, so great was its impact. The baby boom generation was coming of age and acquiring increasing importance.

Rajiv and Catherine shifted from epicentre to epicentre of the counterculture and hippie movement. It was the best and the most happening time to be in the Berkeley/San Francisco area.

The University helped him by making sure that he got accommodation at the International Students House for one year, at the end of the street. Catherine's dorm was walking distance from the Students House.

Both Catherine and Rajiv found that undergrad life at Berkeley was party time. For Rajiv it was a continuation of the time in Delhi in College. They were both good at working quickly to maximise input—absorption and output—meeting the requirements of the University. The overall ethos remained one of fun. They, like others, were swept away by the cultural and sexual revolution, the anti-Establishment struggle against conformity that led to sweeping changes in the way of life and ways of looking at things. Even when powerful people in centres of power fought back and tried to bring back the status quo, ante life was already changing irrevocably. But they, like many others, thought those ideals would never be lost and would last forever.

Rajiv had his head in the clouds, because of the way he was, and this was San Francisco. He was so in love.

On Durant, College and Telegraph—one met people. There were bars, pubs, eateries, the sweet smell of weed everywhere. They were in a place that one only read about, heard about. It was the centre of a worldwide movement of a metamorphosis in values, perceptions, perspective. They had come to the right place. It was a dream come true.

Catherine and Rajiv wandered around Berkeley's localities. Telegraph remained a focal point of revolutionary activity. There was an entrance from Telegraph to campus.

The north side of campus was the Engineering, fancy, Yuppy side. East Berkeley was hills and campus. Guys with money lived in East Berkeley, Berkeley hills were in the background. The hills came down to Campus.

Rajiv and Catherine went up the hills and saw the lights of the City below, scattered below like stars. It was a sight they grew to love. On the south side—there was a party area, music, bums, a parking lot.

Then there was West Berkeley towards the Bay—the Ocean. It had dark, dirty, warehouses. Many Mexicans lived there. Spengers Fish market was popular with everyone, including the crowd from East Berkeley.

The folk culture of the '60s was at its zenith. Joni Mitchell, amongst others, exemplified the sexual independence of the '60s.

Joan Didion's *Slouching Towards Bethlehem* had come out.

A Summer Place still counted as current music and both Catherine and Rajiv loved it. They knew it really applied to them, and it would be wherever they settled down, during their journey together from youthful innocence to adulthood.

Eric Berne's *Games People Play* was still being discussed, as was the much earlier *The Art of Loving* by Erich Fromm. It resonated with the times. The flowers in your hair counter culture was ubiquitous. Most, if not all, students were liberal.

Berkeley was unmistakably at the forefront of student movements in the US. It was no coincidence that student movements worldwide were taking place at the same time and though separated by thousands of miles were unified in thought in many ways. Some of the issues were different and particular or local but many of them were universal and to do with justice and things that were going wrong with humanity, as noted by perceptive observers.[16]

There were student demonstrations in Paris, popular student revolts in Warsaw, in Tokyo, in India and elsewhere. Paris, they had the support of formidable leaders like Sartre, giants of philosophy and the support of workers and many sections of society. There were student leaders like Daniel Cohn-Bendit (Danny the Red). Media coverage at the time highlighted thousands of students demonstrating through Paris.[17]

They ripped up pavement stones. Paris being Paris, the students also had fun and some of the intellectual discussions lasted far into the night, but that didn't take away from the gravitas of their movement. The Fifth republic certainly took it seriously, so much so that they broke up renowned institutions like the Sorbonne, subsequently, into many parts.

The Prague Spring which had started earlier in the year was continuing in May when Catherine and Rajiv were avid watchers still in Delhi.

As a historian observed, the world seemed 'to be changing at unprecedented speed...'[18]

TV, like no other mass media before, brought immediacy and proximity to the images, as perceptively noted by some observers in the media itself. It was the time of Marshal McLuhan's 'The medium is the message'. It was becoming a global village. As someone said, if a butterfly flaps its wings in Siberia, it has an effect on the rain forest in the Amazon.

There was the demonstration effect of and encouragement derived from the success of student movements elsewhere. There were pictures of row upon row of intelligent looking students, with alert expressions, marching with placards, girls in mini-skirts or long dresses, guys—many of them in long hair. It suited them. It was getting to be pervasive for a certain cultural milieu. The Vietnam War and the immediacy of the Draft was one of the major issues. Much of the rest of general opinion was gradually turning against the war but it didn't necessarily lead to all support for the students.

Catherine remarked on Berkeley's flat structure to Rajiv. There was no hierarchy. It was spontaneous, felt by all. It was one of the remarkable things about it.

There were, inevitably, characters. They produced larger than life escapades. Catherine and Rajiv felt a part of them. She was so glad she hadn't chosen a snooty college in the East. She had almost done it, attracted like her parents, by the prestige attached.

Catherine and Rajiv frequently went up the Berkeley hills. They felt the quietness and the breeze. The lights below would be scattered like gold dust.

Once on a hill
'Hey, Mr Tambourine Man,
Play a song for me...'

Bob Dylan's song suddenly came to him.

'Oh, I remember that. That was so beautiful,' said Catherine.

'Was she aware of my reverie and how far away I'd been?' Rajiv thought.

Another time, Rajiv said, 'Life should sparkle like Diamonds…'

Before he could complete, she kissed him and asked, 'Doesn't it?'

Rajiv helped with whatever extra odd jobs came his way in Academia, including in the library. It enabled them to do more things.

They went dancing up at the Fairmont Hotel. He twirled her around. She was light-footed. Her pale coloured dress flowed out as she moved around. The live band caught the mood of this pretty girl and struck up a Waltz. Rajiv could have wanted nothing better. They pirouetted around gracefully. They stopped to sip pink champagne from Moet et Chandon, interspersed with green olives. The lights below from San Francisco Bay were star dust. There was an ethereal quality to it, the evening. Neither of them would forget it.

Rajiv had resented it earlier but was now glad that he had to do a year of undergrad work. There was rebellion everywhere. Had they not been Undergrads they could not have participated the way they did. Not fighting for these things would have meant not fighting for ideals. And what was the World without that?

This time they knew it would be different. This time they would achieve a different world. This time they would make it last. It was in the zeitgeist, the DNA of the times. Dylan sang 'The Times They Are A - Changin'. It was the status quo—the Establishment that had better fall in line.

It would be much more serious the following year when he did what he had come for Grad work. The seminars in each

Semester would require different type of intensive work. Each Semester would carry eight credits. Plus, there would be Exams.

Browsing through music stores, Catherine and Rajiv added to their eclectic collection of 33s and 45s and wrote both their names together on the sleeve along with Berkeley/San Francisco and the month and year.

They went to performances at the Greek Theatre—there were lots of performances, including of music. Amphitheatre 9 reminded Rajiv of Triveni Kala Sangam in Delhi. He had taken Catherine there to a Happening.

They came across psychedelic buses, some of them old Volkswagens. Some young people, including non-students who were hanging around there, lived in moving vans. They went regularly to San Francisco, as did Rajiv and Catherine.

This was a San Francisco, a Haight Ashbury, where sex and rebellion were acclaimed. 'Rebellion was against all forms of conformity and not limited to socially sanctioned, pre-defined definitions of what freedom could safely be,' said Rajiv to Catherine, in agreement with some of the descriptions floating around at the time, one afternoon as they walked past a young girl in a Mini lying on a campus green, making a statement about her freedom. There had to be enlightenment about cultural conformity as well, no matter how well disguised. People were indeed individualistic in terms of being self-sufficient, in terms of being able to look after themselves, in all facets of daily living, repair an assortment of different things. The much-vaunted individualism was there in many respects but there was also social conformity. The present free thinking rebelled against that as well.

The parks had fountains, rose gardens, Bar B Q pits. Catherine taught Rajiv to Barbecue. Young couples would make out on sheets they had laid out in the park.

Catherine went with a group of classmates to Live Oak Park in the north and delved deep into esoteric aspects of Existentialism and felt that she was really living life in the now, doing things that satisfied her and were meaningful. Rajiv was busy that day with classes, else he would have seen how she had flourished in the dialectic. The level of knowledge of some of these students on the subject was quite high, though most of them had not decided on what their Major would be.

In some of the parks young people pitched tents. A couple of stores sold outdoor clothing and tents for travel to India.

They tried their hand at mushroom eating; these were Magical mushrooms—with psychedelic effects—they tasted really bad. Catherine knew how some mushrooms could be really poisonous and worried about that but the sources had good antecedents and she didn't hear about any one getting ill. Nevertheless, the taste and the lingering worry made them stop partaking of this addition to life's richness.

Both Ayesha and Catherine were feminists but in different ways. Ayesha had brought it down to the personal level, to them as a couple. Catherine's view and interpretation was more global. But it was painful to remember Ayesha. He put it out of his head.

On the Berkeley Hills they discovered Indian Rock Park and Catherine shared with Rajiv some of the American poetry that the teacher had talked about in class and that she had enjoyed.

Sometimes in the beautiful blueness of the evenings they listened quietly to Mozart or Chopin or Billy Vaughn and Rajiv saw tears glistening in the corners of her eyes. Catherine and Rajiv identified with 'do your own thing', 'make love not war', 'let it all hang out'.

Sometimes, they joined in the infectious singing and dancing of the Hare Krishnas as they wove their way through the streets.

Rajiv told her about the Bhakti movement and Chaitanya Mahaprabhu and how he would go singing and dancing in the roads of rural Bengal, lined with banana and banyan trees.

'Soon it'll be full moon, Cath,' Rajiv said one day. 'After the drama of the Monsoons and before the winter comes, the Sharad Ritu in India, with its bright, soft golden sunshine, gentle breezes and the trees and grass nourished by the rains a soothing and abundant green. The moonlight is silvery and remarkably luminous. When it gets to be full moon it is called Sharad Poornima. There is a puja in the temple and kheer is placed directly under the moonlight all night.'

'What is kheer?'

'It is made with milk, rice, saffron and sugar or honey. First thing early morning you wake up to it. It has acquired amrit—the nectar of immortality –during the night with the moonbeams.'

Indian spiritualism had really come in a big way to the West in the '60s. The signs of this were already very visible in Delhi, in India, while Rajiv was still in college and when Catherine had come over. That trend continued actively.

Rajiv got a lot of *bhaav*. It was a privilege to walk with him. Catherine felt the same way about India but she couldn't help but notice the attention he got. 'You're from India! Wow! SO cool. Tell us about India... Lot of questions for you... Stories that you would have had... Let's smoke a joint... Listen to this guitar, to Hendrix.'

The vegetarian life style introduced by the Hippies was in sync with the idea of India.

There would be the guy playing guitar till wee hours of the night, the counterpart of the flute player in the distance in India.

The fascination was unmistakable and had seeped deep into

the culture. The entre was automatic. All the more so if one was personable.

India was the *crème de la crème* but it was fashionable, exotic hooking up with a boyfriend/girlfriend with a different ethnicity.

Terms like 'groovy' and 'Far out' were very 60s terms. They were manifestation of that time, as were no bras, long flowing graceful cotton dresses. They evoked Lehengas for Rajiv and Catherine had seen enough of them to know what he meant.

Part of the defining couture of the times were Jeans, multi-coloured Tie dye T-shirts, long cotton summer shirts that looked very comfortable and sophisticated. Some of the girls looked so fetching in them with their vivacity and interesting thought lines.

As the decade progressed, Bell bottoms really became a fashion statement of the late '60s from Carnaby Street, Chelsea and The Beatles sporting them on their cover in England to the Bay Area. At the same time, Feminism, Gloria Steinem and Ms, Germaine Greer and *The Female Eunuch* became well known and well accepted.

The '60s also saw the Environment movement, still nascent but evolving, as thinking people began to see what humans were doing to the world that surrounded them. The media noted that campus had not changed much since World War II. In the '60s it became an entirely different place. It set campus styles in manners, social attitudes, dress and the latest student slang.

Catherine applied for and got a role as one of the editorial team in the *Daily Californian* newspaper. It hardly paid anything but she could express herself and she became well known.

They heard about a big party at San Francisco airport organised by Ginsberg for the founder of Hare Krishna movement, where many groups played, including the Grateful Dead.

The two of them discovered the Sociology of the Frats and

Sororities. There were different Frats. They had lots of activity in the residence Halls near International House. Fraternities were an important part of university life at UC Berkeley, like at many American Universities Frats had parties. Some of them were pretty closed. One had to have an in. There were some wild Frat parties. Rajiv and Catherine wouldn't be interested in all of them.

The Liberal Arts and Pol Science veered towards the Party Frats. There was the Artistic Frat. One particular Frat especially celebrated Halloween. At the first one that the two of them were invited to, they saw students with very intricate costumes. They turned into characters that they wanted to be. One girl came dressed up as an Indian Maharani.

The Jocks had their Sports-oriented Frat. Whilst they both enjoyed Sports, some of them were just Jock, too Jock.

There was an issue of the magazine *Films and Filming* from England. It was *the* magazine for film buffs. It fully reflected the times. It had, of course, French cinema—superb films exploring the human condition. There were a lot of good films coming out of Hollywood, Britain, Czechoslovakia, Italy. It had nice, large, compelling pictures with the most relevant text.

There was a large picture of an actor kissing an actress really passionately. They were in a big kiss. At what point does it cease to be acting and becomes the real thing? They looked like they were really enjoying it. It seemed beyond good acting. They were on a bed and they were sitting up on their knees facing each other. They were without their clothes from the waist downwards. Their thighs, their legs, their stomachs, were right up against each other's. They were jammed so tightly against each other, knees upwards, that it must certainly have meant to convey the impression that they were making love.

It was not possible to be nude and so close and for him not

to be in her, I argued convincingly with Catherine. Catherine sitting right next to me on the mattress of the bed near the window, debated my impression. 'Why,' she said, 'they could be right next to each other, without him going inside her.'

'But they are nude, Catherine—all their clothes there are off. And they couldn't be closer to each other. There is NO space between them. There is not the slightest gap. Their thighs are joined to each other's. Not even air could get in. Can't you see?'

'So what?' Catherine persisted with her viewpoint, smiling charmingly and disarmingly, 'He doesn't have to be in her.'

'Catherine, if you are that close, where is the space for his penis to be, where will it go, where can it be?! It's bound to be very large—he must feel something—it won't be small and limp that it can get crushed against her thigh and be hidden from view. It needs space, a lot of space. Where else can it be in that kind of picture but inside her?'

Catherine was not to be swayed from her views. She conceded that it's *possible* that he's inside her. But it's likely that he's not. These are actors acting out their roles, carrying out their performances. They won't go inside, have actual insertion, penetration. They can't get so carried away. Nor is it necessary.

'Catherine, the more you get into your role the better. There is no prohibition against penetration. In fact, they are supposed to really put themselves into the act. The more they believe it, become it, the more genuine they'll be and the more convincing, believable the portrayal.

'And they are human. They are to lose themselves in their roles, their acting. With that kind of sensory tactile contact, that kind of French kissing—they are bound to be aroused. Feel genuine passion. In which case she'll get wet and he'll become very big. If they are jammed next to each other at the right angle there'll be automatic insertion, whether it's actively planned or not. It's bound to happen—almost certainly.'

Rajiv had not been in his class debating team in school for nothing. He felt that he could win an argument, a debate with anyone—especially if he was convinced of his case. He never gave up.

Catherine did not budge. She was no walkover. There was no other way. Empirical evidence was required. It had to be tried out.

They kissed like that and his thighs were against hers. And without much effort he was in and they were making love. But one swallow doth not a spring make. It had to be tried again and again for the case to be established.

Rajiv looked forward to these experiments with truth. He would feel her naked legs next to his, they would inch up to each other as close as two human beings can possibly get. Their kisses would get more and more open mouthed and po-inng—he'd be in her. Without any conscious attempt. The most important thing was to express the deeply felt love.

So, this happened again and again. Only the kissing, the love making remained. The deep penetration, the abundance of feeling at its profoundest depths.

One exquisite Bay Area evening Rajiv told her that he was going to kiss her from head to foot—every part of her. She had found the idea and its execution very exciting. When he kissed her shoulder blades, the small of her back, each part responded very obviously to the caress. When he kissed her there, she groaned at the salute. 'Hey Jude' played on the radio—unforgettable. It blew their minds.

A few days later as he lay on his back and she was on top of him with her breasts hugging his, she sat up and kissed his swollen swaying member. She was the first person who had kissed him there. She sucked it. He could see her beautiful face. He couldn't believe it was him that this was happening to. He went into the clouds. He loved Catherine so and she was kissing him there. He hadn't even thought of it. This was her own creativity, spontaneity.

6

Catherine met Rajiv for coffee in between classes. He caught the love look in her eyes.

'Cath, I am not all that you think I am.'

'Which is what, prey?' she smiled.

'Many times, I am an inner coward, though I put on an appearance. I hope that others don't see through this.'

Catherine was a different matter. He didn't want to keep a front with her. 'Don't we all feel like that at times, Raj?' she said simply and disarmingly. 'You have moments of courage too, don't you? It's all that one decides in that split second. Sometimes one acts with courage, despite feeling fear, inadequacy, not realising that that's all those are. Nothing long term or worthy of a permanent label.'

'Sometimes, one is able to find this inside and sometimes not', added a reflective Catherine, after a pause. She kissed him and his clouds of self-doubt floated away. Irrelevance.

Catherine and Rajiv discovered that each department had its own requirements. One set of requirements did not necessarily apply to other departments, especially other Divisions.

Grades depended on paper, but also on regular attendance and participation in class. Credits were given for participation in lectures, seminars. This was a general principle. The number of lectures and seminars depended on Departments and could differ from Dept to Dept and across Divisions.

Grads didn't have dorms. International grad students could live for a year in International Students House.

The in between class coffees led to some interesting discussions. Catherine and Raj wondered together—'Americans were the good guys—what happened. Fought the Nazis, were against the harshness of Stalin and Siberian Gulags. But this changed with Hiroshima and deadly bombing of innocent civilians.'

'And now Vietnam is really questionable,' added Catherine.

'Just like NATO, there is SEATO. South Vietnam is in a treaty with the US and several other countries to prevent the takeover by Communists of the South, just like they took over the North. If the North tries to take over the South too, what is wrong with America trying to prevent that?'

'If a NATO ally had been attacked, the US would have been bound to intervene. The Viet Cong was a force created by North Vietnam, it was believed. Not a genuine movement by the South Vietnamese themselves wanting to be Communist.'

'The extent of support for the Viet Cong in South Vietnam seems to have been underestimated, Rajiv. Many of the Viet Cong are not from the North, though it has their support. This is what a lot of them want. And it is questionable if it amounts to a different country, even though politically it is.

'Secondly, and even more importantly, the American public is being greatly misled by McNamara and others at high levels, about how America is winning the war. It is not. The American public wants it over quickly and this is what they keep promising. That it's just over the hill. The Pentagon is complicit in it. For a while, they might have believed it or maybe it was wishful thinking. Independent news media like *Time* backed up that belief. If you read those reports, you genuinely believed that. America was on the verge of winning. They increasingly referred to more and more technological advancement, strategic gains, etc. The deployment of B-52s was going to make such a difference, as were more sophisticated helicopters. Call it hope but it doesn't work like that. It is hard to camouflage the setbacks in the Tet offensive. America is realising that the war is a stalemate, at best. Hard though that might be to believe—a super power against a tiny nation.'

'Hmm—the Vietnamese also defeated the French in Dien Bien Phu in 1954,' Rajiv added thoughtfully.

'The thing that is making it worse is the Draft. Young men who are called up, have to go. They might die or become cripples.'

'LBJ passed the Civil Rights Act of 1964 that outlawed discrimination based on colour or race amongst other things, unequal application of voter registration requirements and segregation. He's an unsung hero, Cath. He has managed billions of dollars in aid to schools for elementary and secondary education and Medicare since 1965—before that poor and elderly had no health insurance. It's still a far cry from Western European welfare societies but a long way from the America before that.

'He pioneered the Voting Rights Act of 1965. I hope it won't be diluted in future by the Courts. The Immigration Reform Act of 1965 was no less momentous. It has scrapped the quota system and has opened the doors for people not just from Western Europe but from Asia, Africa, Latin America and Southern Europe. Time will tell how much this will add to America's openness and greatness. LBJ lacked the charisma, the panache, the elan of someone with movie star looks or personality.'

'Yes, but the disaster of the Vietnam war, Raj...'

'That is why LBJ has not clung to power, unlike many other sitting Presidents with all the advantage that brings.'

'Why do you say that?'

'Presidents in office who have chosen to contest have mostly won, as statistics will reveal. Something wrong with a system that gives such an advantage to someone already in power. And the nomination of their party at the national convention is almost assured. Why should that be so? Why should it not be some other candidate?'

'It's almost a no contest, a charade.'

'Talking of statistics, LBJ's support had fallen to 26 per cent, I believe,' she said.

'No doubt, but that was only early spring. People have bounced back from that. And that was entirely due to the Vietnam war.'

'Yes, but so many lives lost, Rajiv. So much unnecessary killing.' It was clear that the dark shadow of Vietnam eclipsed everything else for her.

'That's an error of judgement and wrong information being fed to the highest levels. That is inexcusable, of course. And nothing justifies even civilians, women and children, being hurt or worse, as vividly brought home by some of the intrepid journalists of *Life* and others in the news media. I agree with you, Catherine, but you still have to look at the man holistically. The momentous changes in some of the domains I've mentioned will change America forever. It won't be the same again.'

'We are talking of two different things, Rajiv—LBJ the man and the Vietnam war.'

'I have looked up to America a lot because of its idealism and what it represents. I still do. But I have been troubled by the bombs on civilians in Hiroshima and Nagasaki.'

'Me too, but they say it ended the Second World War, with all its horrors.'

'Yes, it's presented like that. But was it really necessary, the bombing of innocent people? They would have won without that. Should it not be taken up as a war crime?'

Rajiv had an irresistible urge to kiss her—it was one of the times she was looking most becoming—and forgot what he was going to say.

The next day she was again the clever, urbane, Oscar Wildesque Catherine, testing his wit. He jumped in to the fencing arena. Good practice. Rajiv knew that if something mattered to him he would never give up. He was aware that persistence, determination had helped him overcome obstacles in life. Catherine too persevered with objectives, topics. She had greater self-belief, perhaps a product of her upbringing.

When they encountered problems, Rajiv saw that she was good at solving them. A broad picture person, not a nitty- gritty one, she dealt with essentials. Rajiv complemented that by being both, going into detail where required, even when it was boring.

Despite that he was aware of a nebulous inner feeling that he was faking it at times—he wasn't actually good enough. He tried to understand it, deal with it—where was it coming from, but it persisted.

Catherine was American, but coming from the East Coast 3,000 miles away and with a different history, way of doing things, she and Rajiv both had a journey of discovery together. It didn't feel like the centre of the World as New York had.

Berkeley was small. Soon it became Albany, or Oakland or Emeryville. It was just 17 square miles or so. But it was rich. Shattuck, Durant, Telegraph, Bancroft, University Ave, Walnut St, Allston, Addison, Dwight, Channing Way—all seeped into their subconscious. After some time, they felt comfortable enough to venture on the Bay Bridge descending on to Market St in that fabled city of San Francisco, with all its connotations, for the first time. They ventured on the other side and found that the Univ Ave exit on Highway 80 led straight back to their university. Maybe it would change later on, but right now it didn't disappoint.

Catherine had plenty of time to choose a subject for her major but she was already showing a proclivity for English Literature. In the optionals, for her Freshman year she chose American Literature and the Romantic Period of English Literature.

Rajiv had continued to read a lot of English Literature after school where it had been given a lot of importance. It was one of the subjects he had selected for school leaving. He tried to take it as a subsidiary in College but the Indian system didn't allow for him to take it as the main subsidiary subject in Honours along with Maths. It gave him enough knowledge and interest to have learned discussions with Catherine on what she was writing and reading. He adored Longfellow, amongst other great American writers, he told her. His mother often recited,

> 'Tell me not, in mournful numbers,
> Life is but an empty dream!
> For the soul is dead that slumbers,
> And things are not what they seem.

> Life is real! Life is earnest!
> And the grave is not its goal;
> Dust thou art, to dust returnest,
> Was not spoken of the soul.
> ....

> Art is long, and Time is fleeting,
> ....

Trust no Future, howe'er pleasant!
Let the dead Past bury its dead!
Act,—act in the living Present!
Heart within, and God o'erhead!

Lives of great men all remind us
We can make our lives sublime,
And, departing, leave behind us
Footprints on the sands of time;
....

Let us, then, be up and doing.'
....

Rajiv's subject in St Stephen's College in Delhi for his BA Honours had been Mathematics. He had loved Mathematics in High School, maxing it in the Final School leaving Exam. His mother had loved Geometry in her school and maybe he had inherited this from her. He greatly enjoyed solving riders. This angle is equal to this one, therefore.... The more of a puzzle the better. He would solve it step by step, QED. In Algebra too he went methodically, step by step. From Quadratic Equations to Higher Algebra, Arithmetic too lent itself beautifully to resolution. Don't omit the most obvious step. He took Science in High School and it was fun to get into numericals in Mechanics, Heat, Electricity in Physics. In the Senior year in Berkeley he decided to stick to Mathematics, though he was greatly tempted to do Political Science or International Relations. He really liked all three subjects. With Mathematics he would certainly score higher. He could still consider any of them for his Masters. The American system was renowned for its flexibility and Berkeley even more so.

Catherine was given a place in one of the Residence Halls off Durant. The next year they would move in together. They were clear about wanting to get married, as only the very deeply in love can be, but were not in a hurry. In fact, they both felt that somehow, they were too young for marriage straightaway but not for betrothal. They would decide about when to start living together based on availability, rules, economics and other such practical considerations, irrespective of when they decided to get married.

Soon after their arrival, while the weather was still beautiful, they went to Strawberry Creek, so near Central Berkeley and Downtown Berkeley and having its source in the Berkeley hills, on one of their first picnics. They were told that it was one of the main reasons the University was set up at this location. 'It was set up in 1868 and we are in 1968, exactly a 100 years ago', said Catherine, as they trudged through the paths. In a thicket, she suddenly turned around and kissed him. It made everything worth it. He wanted nothing more at that moment.

Rajiv started discovering what excellent wines California had. He had only known of French, Italian and other European wines. He bought a chilled Chardonnay, Catherine packed a picnic basket of Cobb Salad and Avocado Toast, neither of them familiar with Californian food and both of them wanting to go local.

Rajiv came across the Men's Tennis Courts, very centrally located, as he tried to settle down. He found some good hitting partners. But the surface was very strange. The gravel court was much more unpredictable, the bounce was often not the same and it could make the ball spin or slow down. That made the game much more challenging. The grass he played on at the Club was even more like that. The game was originally Lawn Tennis, he reminded one of the guys on the Courts. Rajiv played at a very good level. That was one of the things he had in common with Catherine. Gravel and grass were both much easier on the body, especially in terms of shocks to the head and the effect on knees. But after the initial bit of settling down and finding his feet, he missed playing with Catherine and found Courts where he could play with her. Their time tables were different, hers that of a Freshman, his that of a Senior.

The Rotunda remained a silent, significant witness to the momentous revolutions taking place.

Dylan had already sung songs like 'Blowin' in the Wind' and performed in the Bay Area, as had David Simon. Jefferson Airplane sang about Revolution, as did The Beatles. It was the time of Simon and Garfunkel's 'Mrs Robinson'.

In America and in particular, the Berkeley/San Francisco area, were spearheading what became known worldwide as the '60s counterculture and the effect of which very rapidly percolated, especially to the urban middle and upper classes everywhere.

America saw Integrated schools by September 1968.

Movie stars David Newman, Marlon Brando had already come to California in the first half of the '60s in support of non-discrimination in housing. Influential figures like Joan Baez, who sang in support of the late '60s movements. She had already come to the Free Speech Movement rally in 1964.

The impact would be felt greatly in the times to come, the agitating students knew.

The confrontation at Sheraton Palace with the Hotel Owners Association about equal employment opportunities had been unexpectedly successful.

Catherine and Rajiv were active participants. The idealism and hope of fellow students for a better world was contagious. They were both interested in their subjects and neither of them neglected their studies. The Professors were inspiring and the student movements found an echo in their own way of thinking.

The Administration, however, was inimical. On Bancroft and Telegraph tables were barred. It was a lifeline of the campus political activity, as the media reported. The Administration said no non-Campus issues could be raised. Political activity was barred. University students were joined by thousands of Berkeley High School students in solidarity. [19]

Sproul Hall was at the centre of protests. Students were bumped down the stairs by the police, Catherine and Rajiv amongst them. This was so far from Rajiv's image of America.

Much to the horror of her upper-class East Coast family, Catherine actually got locked in for a night along with several other students when she resisted. What sort of company was their daughter keeping? They almost flew down to rescue her and bring her back to the Ivy League where she belonged. But they were equally shocked that this could happen in America, the land of freedom, liberty, democracy. What had their daughter done wrong to be locked away like a criminal? Did this mean she had a "record" now, in American parlance?

The Free Speech Movement started earlier continued unabated. The faculty came out in favour.

Joan Baez came.

The *nouvelle vague* was here too in the thinking of the *avant garde*. There was freedom of how one looked at things, of imagination.

It was widely reported in the media that the Love Ins, the sexual freedom, the cultural revolution, the attitude towards material success as the most important goal in life, were part of this phenomenon. It was unbelievable change at a velocity that one could hardly comprehend. The students passed out flowers, symbols of how to live differently, how to change society. The flower culture that came from Hippies, transformed culture by actually living it differently. Rajiv and Catherine couldn't agree more. It was a new world in the new world, parallel to the existing one.

They saw first-hand how civil disobedience (with antecedents not just of Thoreau and Gandhi but going far back) was one of the means being widely used. Students like Catherine and Rajiv, from entitled backgrounds, began to view themselves too as controlled, with the change of lens.

The students saw that these were big things happening in the America of 1968 and it (and indeed the World) was being profoundly affected. Rajiv and Catherine believed, like many others, that it would be a permanent change.

The Establishment too was formidable and equally determined about the status quo. They had to concede that the aftershocks of all this would remain but they would dilute the change over the years to the extent they could.

Rajiv thought the Police would be friendly, were there to help them but to his surprise, he found that they didn't seem to have that attitude, to be trained like that. What was the ethos being imparted to them? There seemed to be a harshness about them.

He mentioned it to other students, who told him—'Once they question you for anything, you are in their custody. You are assumed to be in the wrong.'

Another student from England expatiated—'I'm no Law student but they use strange terms like felony and misdemeanour as it suits them, distinctions which don't exist elsewhere.'

Another cohort said, 'Like your car licence plate has expired and you didn't even know about it or you exceed the speed limit and instead of stopping you speed up to escape, police can still throw you on to the pavement, face down, no matter how dirty it is, put your hands behind your back and handcuff you like the most primitive and totalitarian of societies, their operating procedure is the same. They can hit you when you've been thrown to the ground, and use obscure terms like they want you to be lying prone.'

A girl from L.A. added police justified blatant murder by calling it self-defence and got away with it. 'If you have an unloaded gun, if you go for your wallet to show your ID—will say thought was going for his gun. They are like the Broederbond in South Africa—they will defend and support each other at any cost, no matter how obvious the wrong.'

8

Every time Rajiv saw Catherine, he was lost in her persona, her charm, her less than perfect beauty, which added to who she was and which was perfect for him. He looked at her eyes and felt like swimming in their depth. He imagined her kiss and felt weak in the knees. He imagined her touch and felt dizzy.

This was the person who embodied the pleasantness, the romance, the dreaminess of America, the America of his imagination. The lovely person he would meet in a pastoral American meadow with snow- white mountains in the depth of vision.

Catherine and Rajiv went past a small art film house and impulsively ducked into a matinee of a Peter Sellers film. Catherine had always found Peter Sellers extremely funny. Both of them laughed so hard they couldn't stop. Rajiv remembered times in life when he was tense or upset about something, he would end up laughing extra at anything that provided comic relief. He shared this thought with Catherine; she looked thoughtful and then agreed.

After wandering around the whole day on foot, Rajiv didn't particularly feel like going out. Catherine was tired too, so they decided to relax chez Catherine, who put on a motley collection. Don Mclean came on with 'Till Tomorrow' and 'Winterwood'. Rajiv loved this and almost the whole collection of music in the *American Pie* album.

Then it was Leonard Cohen with 'Suzanne'.

'What are you thinking?' she asked.

'Oh, nothing,' he said.

'C'mon, out with it,' she laughed.

'I was just thinking that this was a 'Suzanne' like setting ...'

'Just like it was 'Norwegian Wood' the other day?' she interrupted.

'Hey, are you a mind reader, Lady Anne, or what?'

'*C'est pas si difficile,*' she said, breaking into French. 'It was quite obvious,' she smiled.

'The setting or its coming to my mind?'

'The setting and therefore the congruence with the songs and it occurring to you.'

'It's not quite congruent. Besides, you're not Suzanne.'

'Ah, *mais c'est qui,* Suzanne. Anyone could be Suzanne. Besides, when, pray, is it congruent? At best situations, approximate.'

'Hey, I never knew you spoke French as well.'

'Oh, I took it in school in New York.'

After a pause, 'What do you mean, anyone could be Suzanne?'

'C'mon, you understand. It does not require annotation. Do you know that "Norwegian Wood" is not, in fact, set in one?'

> 'I looked around
> And noticed there wasn't a chair
> ....
> I, sat on the bed
> Drinking her wine
> ....
> We, talked until two
> And then she said
> It's time for bed'
> ....

There was a companionable pause.

'I have excellent French Pinot Noir. Should we have some?' he asked.

'Yeah, let's. Gosh, I'm living these few days so intensively. As if there's no tomorrow.'

'Isn't that the only way to live? Not necessarily at the same scorching pace and not with anxiety but intensely, so as to make the most of every moment of the journey.'

'What about the worry habit?'

'Habits can be changed with practice and will power. Why lose the present also?'

Catherine wasn't the only beautiful girl but there was something very attractive about her and she was noticed. Jeff and Mark vied for a place next to her.

Jeff engaged her in conversation after class and after a couple of times, asked her to have a coffee with him nearby. She hesitated, but it was just coffee; his company was stimulating and conviviality was an essential part of life. If he asked her if she had a boyfriend, she would, of course say, but he didn't. Interaction with different ideas, different thoughts made her all the more interesting. She was witty and could be very quick at repartee, many people including Rajiv had told her. Such classmates helped her thrust and parry and keep in good shape. There might have been an overlap with flirting but she was so young and it was fun.

Jeff was good looking in a Pat Booneish kind of way, with the early '60s look modified to a late '60s one. He was very taken with English Literature and would probably take it as his major. He knew that she was going with Rajiv but couldn't help but be strongly attracted to her. Rajiv was much more Senior anyway and he could show-off in class in front of her. Catherine was attracted too but tried to keep it within boundaries. She knew that at this phase in life people were often at a stage of exploration, they were finding themselves, not just what they sought in their partners and relationships could change.

Rajiv believed that she was faithful, loyal. Was she capable of being tempted? If that question arose, he put it in the recesses of his mind and did not acknowledge it. Sometimes, when he came to meet her after class, the way she would be talking to Jeff.

There were some get togethers just for their class. There was a lot of bonhomie, there was dancing too. Jeff made it a point to dance with her and tried to monopolise her. He was good at moving to the rhythm and at leading. After a while she would say thank you and sit down or go and join a group of people laughing or Mark, in turn, would cut in.

Mark was good at many sports, especially tennis and cycling. He was also into fitness and worked out regularly in the gym. As a result, he had the build of a jock, though he wasn't quite a jock. He was part of the Sports Frats and went to their dos. No accounting for tastes, an English classmate remarked to Rajiv, seeing how girls were attracted to him. He used Catherine's love of tennis to invite her regularly for matches and when she didn't have time just for some knocks. They would cycle together to the tennis courts and he'd invite her for a Strawberry milk shake after that. His Tennis was also cerebral, based on clever angles and placements, not just on hard hitting from the baseline. He kept changing his tactics, mixed and matched, kept his opponent guessing. Catherine was a good match for him, blunting his attack with good returns and having strategies of her own.

One glorious Bay Area early evening, Catherine had just defeated Mark. She was flushed from playing and looked utterly desirable in her white Tennis outfit. Mark had a strong urge to jump over the net and kiss her but restrained himself. It was getting more and more difficult.

Creativity thrived in the San Francisco/Berkeley area. Rajiv noticed how much colour there was. It reminded him of India. Psychedelia *par tout*.

John Fogerty, who co-founded the Credence Clearwater Revival, was there. Fantasy Records that signed them on were in Berkeley itself. There were people from many walks of life, like one of the co-founders of Intel. The culture of the times also produced *2001: A Space Odyssey*, amongst other things.

Martin Luther King, the non-violent follower of civil disobedience, inspired by Thoreau and Gandhi, in a significant *gifle* to civilisation, was assassinated in April 1968; Rajiv and Catherine had not yet met. In Berkeley, organisations like SAVE (Students Against Violence Everywhere) were rising.

They were in Delhi when Robert Kennedy was assassinated— he was leading the Democratic primaries after Johnson announced he would not stand. Hubert Humphrey became the Democratic nominee. There was civil unrest. August 1968 saw the Democratic Convention in Chicago and the brutality just outside. Mayor Richard Daley came down hard.

Bill Clinton and, ironically, George Bush, Trump were all students in the late '60s, the latter two the anti-thesis of what the decade represented.

'How come America, a nation of immigrants, was so parochial, so naïve in its approach to the rest of the world,' thought Rajiv aloud to Catherine. 'How come the melting pot, which by definition should have been otherwise, had become insular.' She hadn't thought of it that way but then came up with a plausible reason. Trust her. 'The immigrants had come to a continent—a very large, virgin place, with an abundance of natural resources and land for farming; as America became more and more rich and powerful, with its immense wealth and military power, it strode the world stage like a Colossus, as it were, it looked more and more inwards. The need to look outside became less and less important.'

As the early '60s became the late '60s, both halves of '60s, decades in themselves in terms of change, it became even more of an anomaly. Even legends like Frank Sinatra had openly questioned it. The students were appalled at propaganda films like *Operation Abolition*.

Reagan, who as Governor of California, determined to ruthlessly stomp out the counter culture, came down with such a heavy hand on the protesting students in Berkeley, was the main challenger to Nixon in the 1968 Republican primaries. One worse than the other.

Nixon assumed the presidency in 1968 anyway, successfully misusing the law-and-order platform and the fear of taxation against Hubert Humphrey. Humphrey lost to Nixon, who promised stability, without addressing the root cause of social unrest (much like Trump in current times). J. Edgar Hoover as head of FBI had enormous power, which he did not hesitate with the utmost ruthlessness to crush anything he didn't approve of. The triumvirate of Nixon, Reagan and Hoover at the Federal, State and Police Intelligence levels made for power centres that cared just for their ends. SLATE, the student organisation against McCarthyism, had been successfully dissolved just a couple of years ago.

Rajiv tried not to get disillusioned about America. What place would be left, then, as a perfect place?

The atmosphere in the universities and in particular at Berkeley, remained politically vibrant and students quite aware and knowledgeable. The faculty came out in support of the students. The student structure was non-hierarchical. It had spontaneous large-scale participation.

The Mexico Olympics in October 1968 saw two black athletes with raised fists on the podium when the American national anthem was being played.

The Berkeley students supported the Civil Rights Movement. This was also the time in Berkeley of CORE—Co-operation with Civil Rights.

Around the same time, the Black Panthers were founded in the Bay Area after the assassination of Malcolm X and as analysed by some of the media, fed up of oppression subtle and overt, carried weapons openly. The right to bear arms was a fundamental right in America. For a while they were successful but the police managed to throw them all in prison, backed by similar minded courts on jail terms that implausibly had no relationship to the human life span.

They were put on trial for their political beliefs, successfully creating a climate of fear for those who dared to cross a certain line, in this country, whose quintessence was meant to be freedom.

9

Catherine got some eminent professors. She was a well-known authority on her period. Catherine was in awe of her reputation. She told Rajiv excitedly about them. Rajiv laughed—'They may be stars but you don't have to be starry eyed about them.'

One of them was Prof. Anne Wedgewood, who taught English Literature of the Romantic period. Catherine loved that period.

Some of the Faculty gave her good advice. American education all about choice—they said, extraordinary choice—more choice than anywhere else. Part of that choice is that one doesn't have to feel pressure to decide Major right in the beginning, even if in admission processes they ask for personal insight to know you better.

Catherine was pleasantly surprised to see that she knew a lot of things being discussed in the English class. She had adored Wordsworth, Shelley, Keats and Coleridge from school itself. Byron she was less familiar with. Her hand would frequently shoot up. A few times, she found herself adding to what the teacher had said.

After some time, she noticed that Anne had started cutting her short. 'Fair enough,' thought Catherine. Her time is limited and she has to cover a certain amount of material during each class.

As the trend continued and some of Anne's remarks became sharper in front of the whole class, Catherine wondered—'Oh gosh! I hope she didn't think I was trying to show-off.' She had nothing but respect for Anne's learning. It couldn't be that Anne was jealous of Catherine or had otherwise taken a dislike to her. Professors were above that, especially someone of Anne's stature. It was inconceivable.

Some of the girls in class she had become friendly with proposed this as a plausible explanation. She was vivacious, attractive, she got a lot of attention. Catherine tried to talk to Anne but she was distant and formal.

Catherine worked hard on the papers she submitted even when it meant not going out on some evenings planned with Rajiv or coming back earlier than warranted from a dinner out, in which she was having a lovely time. She knew some of the papers she submitted were very good but was amazed to see the B minus grades on them. She showed the paper to another teacher, John Welsh, who had come from being a Don at Oxford. He seemed open and friendly and she felt at ease enough to ask him. She had seen his face in the University brochure and been inspired. He said these are very good papers. He would have given an A+ on them, but he was circumspect in not saying anything about Anne or her marking. 'You just have to bite the bullet and carry on,' he added.

As the term progressed the problems with Prof. Ann, instead of diminishing, worsened, though Catherine tried her best to smoothen things out.

Class participation was encouraged and a percentage of the total grade was given for that. Many points occurred to Catherine. She knew they were important and pertinent. She had questions too. She put her hand up. The point was more important than the person. She hoped that Ann would deal with it on its substance. But Ann dealt with it summarily, not really answering the question.

A pretty girl, Debbie's class participation was high. It became obvious that she was used to being top of the class from wherever she had come. To her dismay, she found that Debbie too perceived her as a rival, whom she would not be friends with. There were a bunch of girls from her school in the local area, who were part of her gang. She, from the East, was an outsider and they resented her social strata. They would whisper and giggle and look at her sometimes when she passed; they would laugh uproariously at Anne's remarks. 'Puerile',—she thought. 'Do they not realise that they are no longer in School but in University?'

The situation became disagreeable enough for her to mention it to Rajiv. 'Why, for God's sake,' she asked Rajiv. 'But what does she have against me?'

'Whatever you do, Catherine, do not think it is some shortcoming in you. Do not start putting yourself down or blaming yourself. One can easily fall into that. What is wrong with me? I must be doing something wrong. There are other Professors who like you, besides, who don't feel the same way. Your grade point average is still good. Besides, there are always some bad eggs everywhere, in one way or another. There are lots of students who like you, think highly of you, Debbie notwithstanding. In your previous school, you didn't experience this. Apart from that gang, the rest of the class must be supportive. Don't you find that?'

The quality of Anne's lectures was very good, personal problems notwithstanding. She loved the poems. They would remain.

She would read them again and again and her mind would soar along with them.

Wordsworth and his *Ode to Immortality*

> 'There was a time when meadow, grove, and
> stream,
> The earth, and every common sight,
> To me did seem
> Apparelled in celestial light.
> ....
>
> Our birth is but a sleep and a forgetting:
> The Soul that rises with us, our life's Star,
> Hath had elsewhere its setting,
> And cometh from afar:'
> ....

Tintern Abbey and his Pantheist poems where he sees God all around him. Very close to Hinduism, interjected Rajiv, when she discussed it with him. It sees God in every tree and every bird, flower or rock.

She really liked his bunch of shorter poems...

My Heart Leaps Up

> 'My heart leaps up when I behold
> A rainbow in the sky:
> So was it when my life began;
> So is it now I am a man.'
> ....

The Lucy poems

> 'In one of those sweet dreams I slept,
> Kind Nature's gentlest boon!
> And, all the while, my eyes I kept
> On the descending moon.'

She imagined him composing them as he wandered over hill and dale...

Daffodils

> 'I wandered lonely as a cloud
> That floats on high o'er vales and hills,
> When all at once I saw a crowd,
> A host, of golden daffodils;
> Beside the lake, beneath the trees,
> Fluttering and dancing in the breeze.'

It reminded Rajiv also of Tagore and *Geetanjali*; he read it out to her ...

Little Flute

> 'Thou hast made me endless, such is thy
> pleasure. This frail
> vessel thou emptiest again and again, and fillest
> it ever with fresh life.
>
> This little flute of a reed thou hast carried over
> hills and dales,
> and hast breathed through it melodies eternally
> new.'

Catherine talked about *The Prelude*, a poem in many parts captivating, beautiful, about the poet, his life. How the idea of Growth of a Poet's mind was crucial to it, how his idea of the Epic was different from that of Milton.

Rajiv had heard the quote: 'But to be young was very heaven'.

Wordsworth initially planned to work with Coleridge on *The Prelude*, they intended it to surpass Milton's *Paradise Lost* in length.

'It too is beautiful, Rajiv, of a different period, of course.'

'They also serve who only stand and wait,' he remembered.

'It's from the sonnet *When I consider how my light is spent*,' she said.

The Romantic Poets were greatly influenced by the French Revolution just across the Channel, as were other intellectuals as well as the Polity in England. Liberty, Equality, Fraternity, especially the equality of all, found great resonance. This was especially so with the French Revolution at its commencement before it got very bloody.

Another thing, she continued, they strongly espoused was that poetry should be the language and subject of the common man.

The Polity wanting to pre-empt the possibility of an uprising in England came up with Reform bills over time.

Wordsworth and Coleridge came out with a collection of poems, *Lyrical Ballads*. This included Coleridge's famous The *Rime of the Ancient Mariner*.

'Oh, I know that one,' exclaimed Rajiv. 'Another beautiful one in it is The *Nightingale*.'

Coleridge's poems dealt with the supernatural also— *Christabel, Ode to Dejection, Kubla Khan* (where there is this fabled place, Xanadu).

'Rajiv, I think Wordsworth and Shelley are my favourites amongst the Romantics, though I like them all.'

Shelley's poems were a lot to do with nature, with the free spirit. Shelley famously wrote that poets were the unacknowledged legislators of the world. His poems exemplified life's variety—'Is the million-coloured bow'.

She read out his *Ode to the West Wind* in her auditioning voice:

'O wild West Wind, thou breath of Autumn's
being,
Thou who didst waken from his summer dreams
The blue Mediterranean, where he lay,
. . . .
So sweet, the sense faints picturing them!
. . . .
If I were a swift cloud to fly with thee;
. . . .
O Wind,
If Winter comes, can Spring be far behind?'

Here's another: *To a Skylark*

'We look before and after,
And pine for what is not:
Our sincerest laughter
With some pain is fraught;
Our sweetest songs are those that tell of saddest
thought.
. . . .
Teach me half the gladness
That thy brain must know,
Such harmonious madness
From my lips would flow
The world should listen then, as I am listening
now.'

And *The Cloud*

'I bring fresh showers for the thirsting flowers,
From the seas and the streams;
I bear light shade for the leaves when laid
In their noonday dreams.

From my wings are shaken the dews that waken
The sweet buds every one.'

'Exquisite,' said Rajiv. 'Let's go and sit on the grass in that park. It brings to mind Kalidas' *Meghdoot*. I'll see if I can get a good translation from Sanskrit to English to read out to you. We'll have champagne and green olives and you can lie on the grass and put your head on my lap. Megh is cloud in Sanskrit and Doot is messenger.'

Life in St Stephen's had meant wide reading for Rajiv and his College mates. Such was the ethos of the College that students vied with each other on being well read, having an interest in a variety of subjects, especially to do with the Arts. But when Catherine read out and narrated some of these to him, he enjoyed it so much, got into it so much, that he seriously considered adding it as a subject at this late stage, even though it was far removed from his chosen subjects. It opened whole new worlds for him and her thought processes gave it that much more depth and background.

'Keats' sonnets are so evocative, Rajiv. You may know some like Keats' *Ode to Beauty* (titled *Endymion*)—'A thing of beauty is a joy forever …' etc. Here, I'll read out extracts from others. Actually, I may well know some of his stuff by heart.'

'May I put my head in your lap, Cath?'

'Sure,' she said.

'Blue! Gentle cousin of the forest green,
Married to green in all the sweetest flowers,
Forget-me-not,– the blue-bell,—and, that queen
Of secrecy, the violet...'
………………..

Ode on a Grecian Urn

> 'Bold Lover, never, never canst thou kiss,
> Though winning near the goal yet, do not grieve;
> She cannot fade, though thou hast not thy bliss,
> For ever wilt thou love,'

> 'But thou, thou shalt have my kiss', she said,
> bending down and kissing him.
> 'Ah, happy, happy boughs! That cannot shed
> Your leaves, nor ever bid the Spring adieu;'
> ....

To Autumn

> 'Where are the songs of spring? Ay, Where are
> they?
> Think not of them, thou hast thy music too,—
> ....
> The red-breast whistles from a garden-croft;
> And gathering swallows twitter in the skies.'

10

Both of them liked the Marina and started meeting there to have an aperitif and watch the spectacular sunset on the Bay, after the day's curriculum was over. The golden light imbued their moods, though it didn't prevent a quarrel from time to time, often over something trivial. Inevitable that the fun times be interspersed with that. They would both quickly get over it, Catherine faster than Rajiv. They had to look at each other, at the other's eyes and one or the other would start smiling.

The first time Rajiv went there he asked for a sweet sherry. The young girl looked puzzled—'What's that, cherry?' she asked, drawing out the e. 'No, no, sherry.' She asked a colleague who came and repeated the cherry sequence in exactly the same way.

'Sherry and port, you know. They drink it often in England. You must have seen in movies or on TV. Sherry comes from Spain.'

It didn't bring enlightenment. He went to the bar counter, thinking he'll give up after this. He got a shortish English bartender who knew instantly and smiled in recognition of a kindred spirit, as if to say—what you are doing here in these Badlands.

'Go West, young man,' Rajiv said, reading his thoughts.

Catherine came just in time to see the young man smiling.

In the non-commercial Berkeley Arts Centre for local artists, they had a difference of opinion, which turned into an argument about some of the paintings and drawings. Catherine liked many of them. Rajiv said he wasn't inspired. They were neither pleasing to the eye nor stimulating.

'You cannot confine yourself to the conventional, Rajiv, nor to the obviously commercially appealing.'

'I agree but I am not. I don't find anything appealing in them. Must I like them just because they are from local artists and not represented in commercial galleries? There has to be an intrinsic appeal for me, irrespective of commercial success.'

'Look how imaginative this one is.'

'What is imagined must stimulate me or set me thinking in some way or it must please me.'

Afterwards, neither of them even remembered which paintings/drawings they were arguing about.

Sometimes, after a particularly bad argument, he told himself he wasn't here just because of her. He was here because of his education.

They saw some lovely revival house films at the UC Theatre but Catherine would complain that she missed some important scenes as Rajiv would turn sideways and keep kissing her.

Rajiv saw how everything was indeed big in America, like in the song in *West Side Story* and distances were meant to be traversed. Eisenhower had made the roads very large and very good. Fit for the ideals of the Pentagon—for the military to race down, if need be. But it was ordinary citizens who drove everywhere, vast distances, like in no other place. The automobile industry was a key industry for America, with a very strong lobby. Regular cars were cheap, Rajiv saw, though there was no end to how fancy automobiles could get. Second-hand cars were even cheaper.

A fellow student was selling his car as he had saved up for a better one. The source was reliable and the price was attractive. Rajiv had learnt the art of making some extra money by helping out with the teaching assistantships. Many students did something or the other to get some extra money.

He became the proud owner of an easily manoeuvrable Volkswagen Beetle, enough for Catherine and him.

Rajiv took her to the Japanese tea garden in San Francisco. The flowers gave them spiritual nourishment. They sipped tea in the Tea House. Rajiv taught her Transcendental Meditation. Simple but effective. She read out from some of the transcendentalists to him. Catherine drove on the way back. They came to a little-known ridge like place overlooking the Bay. They often came back here on visits to the City. It became their place.

Once they played 'hookey' from class and felt deliciously wicked. They stumbled on the Eucalyptus Grove not far from the Life Sciences Building. The afternoon light on the tree trunks was worthy of an impressionist painting. *'Dejeuner sur l'herbe,'* he said and produced a ham and cheese sandwich each.

'One day we'll see the original,' she said in Paris but Rajiv's mind was on Catherine. Every opportunity he stole a kiss and she said tch, tch, tch in protest. Another time, after class, they decided to go to the Hearst Museum of Anthropology, in campus. Rajiv had to behave. Catherine looked at him sternly. They were too many attendants about.

They went to San Francisco. It was the best time to be there, though they/ nobody knew it then. Haight Ashbury, with all that it connoted, was at its climax. The Bay Bridge was ordinary looking. Something iconic should have connected Berkeley with San Francisco, like the Golden Gate bridge.

They went to Love Ins. It was hard to believe but they got swept away by it. It seemed the most natural thing in the world. There was something about it. They went again and again.

It was the height of flower power and Scott McKenzie's 'If you are going to San Francisco ...' 'If New York was the centre of the World, this was the centre of this new movement, this new way of being,' aptly wrote someone in the media—'the area managed to hold the Beautiful People long enough for it to become part of folklore.'

'Time, time, time,

See what's become of me ...' Rajiv started the Simon and Garfunkel song and Catherine joined him.

Allen Ginsberg was there. He had been friends with Jack Kerouac. It was widely acknowledged that the present (genuinely) individualistic and socially non-conformist movements had a connection with the earlier Beatnik movement, which also had a lot to do with the Bay Area. In the frontline of some of the student protests, he chanted *om namah shivaya* to the cops. Since communism was a bad word in America, Ginsberg objected: 'I am not, as a matter of fact, a member of the Communist party, nor am I dedicated to the overthrow of the U.S. government or any government by violence ... I must say that I see little difference between the armed and violent governments both Communist and Capitalist that I have observed'. [20] Ginsberg travelled to several communist countries to promote free speech.

The status quo had felt so threatened that the Customs, whose duty it is to protect against contraband goods, had in earlier years confiscated his poem *Howl*, in which '... he decried what he saw as the destructive forces of capitalism and conformity in the United States'.[21]

In a similar vein, The Beatles came out with 'Back in the U.S.S.R'.

11

Catherine and Rajiv attended University lectures outside their subjects when time permitted. There was a lecture that interested Catherine, on Existentialism beyond Sartre and Camus. They sank gratefully into their chairs and listened. He slipped his hand into hers. 'I wanna hold your hand'.

Catherine's lodging was not far. The afternoon was unexpectedly bright.

'For some reason, William Saroyan—"Boys and Girls Together", came to mind.'

'I remember liking that,' Catherine replied.

'The sun is as bright as the Venetian one,' Rajiv continued. 'You need Venetian blinds for this kinda golden sun.'

'This afternoon, it's more like Rome,' she said.

Rajiv's chain of thought took him to Alberto Moravia. He had enjoyed the sensuousness with an underlying sense of wickedness that he had managed to convey. Somehow, the seduction scenes were always in the hot Roman afternoons. He hadn't read him in such a long while. He shared his thoughts with Catherine. What better time, her smile seemed to say, as much as you can gauge the mystery behind any woman's smile.

Catherine turned back and kissed him, diagonally. He spun her around and their kiss escalated into an explosive kiss. Her chin was pressed against his. There were kiss lines on their cheeks. Its tempo kept changing from feverish to full-mouthed to semi-open. The bright and golden Moravian light poured down upon them. He felt her saliva as he inserted his tongue and explored her mouth. The blood rushed to his head. The kiss between every couple is different, unique. Her top tightly hugged her body, deliciously outlining her contours.

They moved away from each other slightly and he put his hands on her shoulders. It fitted perfectly. He kept both his hands there as they kissed. It added dimensions to their kiss, which was already rich, with multiple strands.

'Archaeological,' he mumbled in-between the kiss. Catherine laughed in her throat. Time is just a measurement. Its depth and longevity keep changing. It is linked to so many things. It is certainly not one dimensional, Rajiv found himself thinking. He shrugged whilst kissing her.

'What was that?' she asked. '*Qu'est que tu penses?* A penny for them.'

'A kiss, not a mere penny.'

'Insatiable,' she said, 'only after you tell me.'

He told her briefly. He was surprised to hear his voice. It sounded thick with desire. It felt like he had phlegm in his mouth.

'Time is relative. We all know that. Time as it's divided is just an arbitrary measure devised by man,' she said, echoing his thoughts.

'At one level, it's fine, it serves a purpose. But it gives no idea of the qualitative dimension of what it feels like. When days are eventful and intensely lived, you don't know where they've gone. They pass in an instant. At the same time, because so much is happening, it seems like the first thing you did was such a long time back. The beginning was so long ago.'

'When you are completely in the moment, time seems to stand still.' He took up where she left off.

'When feelings get accumulated, it seems so long.'

'You mean desire?' she said, tongue in cheek.

He gave her a whopper of a kiss. It became a double suction kiss. Rajiv broke off to continue.

'When you are waiting for something to come through, it seems like ages. Or when something is unpleasant, a few minutes seem like a lot, like a dentist drilling...'

'Yet in an exam, which would not be called pleasant by most, time just flies,' she said. This seemed like too long an interruption. 'Stop talking about time,' she said. Their mouths got clasped together. They remained like that for a long time.

He went and peed noisily. Czech movies being produced in the '60s came to mind. They were so good. Maybe adversity inspired, sparked extraordinary creativity. Was it a movie of Milos Forman, Jiri Menzel, one of the other well-known directors of the time? There was a movie he had seen with her, where a young man comes home late at night, after partying with his girlfriend, and then pees noisily into the pot. It reminded him so much of himself. It had him in splits, the way he did it. Catherine kept shushing him.

'Czech cinema is something else. I hope it is able to sustain its creativity without stepping on the toes of the Communist regime, like it has managed so far.'

Some birds glided high above in the blue evening sky. The movie *Diary of Anne Frank* flashed through his mind. He had seen it as a child and been greatly affected by it. He read the book afterwards and as is often the case, liked it even more. Seeing the sky through the window reminded him. In the movie, the window was tiny in the hidden attic. The actress was so pretty—who was it? Millie Perkins? 'Look at the sky, Peter,' she said, showing him the sky and the clouds and the birds circling way up above. For days afterwards, he went around singing 'Look at the sky Peter', a tune based on the movie, that he'd made up.

'Snap out of your reverie,' Catherine said, kissing him very softly, closed mouthed. It was no less sensuous.

'If you kiss me like that, you'll put me in one.'

'Even after all the kissing we've done?' she said, smiling flirtatiously.

'Stop it.'

'Dizzy, My head is turning, I'm so dizzy, Dizzy …' played somewhere in some realm.

12

Walking down Allston Way, Catherine said, 'Rajiv, I overheard you saying to your classmate, Wyatt, the other day that power distribution seems imbalanced in the US Legislature. What did you mean?'

'It seems to me the Upper House, the Senate, has too much power. In most democracies, if at all there is an Upper House, it's the Lower House that has the most power. Here it seems to be the other way about. It is only the Senate that has the power to confirm the appointment of the judges of the Supreme Court, which are lifelong appointments, and other Federal judges. Few countries appoint them for life—it makes this power all the more potent.'

'Snow on, I follow your drift.'

'Supreme Court Judges are enormously powerful, their judgements become like law and they represent the third branch of Government in the US balance of power. Senators are elected for six long years versus just two for Congressmen—the direct representatives of their district. Not even four or five years, like in most countries. Only the Senate gives consent to international treaties, confirms Cabinet Secretaries appointed by the President as well as Ambassadors.'

'I have believed in American democracy being great, Cath, since I was in school, but every system needs constant reform and change as Society evolves and is transformed by rapidly changing Technology and a growing human population. Benjamin Franklin, for instance, would have been the first to say so. The Constitution, for example, written by the Founding Fathers, no matter how well thought out at the time, cannot become sacrosanct, immutable. The odd amendment now and then cannot suffice or be a substitute for a reset, for a complete rethinking or starting from scratch. It is just tinkering, whereas sometimes it is easier and better to have a tabula rasa, as architects sometimes feel about buildings.'

'Hmmm…and some of these Amendments actually detract from the liberty of others, though they are ironically portrayed as the liberty to carry arms, as in the Second Amendment.'

'As Shaw said, something like your freedom to swing your stick ends at the tip of my nose,' said Catherine, getting into the topic.

The misuse by some judges of the intention of the Constitution, even though it dates back to 1787, in a society where things change the fastest and he had heard people say, 'Oh, that's so last month.' Why sanctify the original intention—whatever that might be—and use it to justify inherent Conservatism?

'And what I have been coming across on TV and the newspapers here, Cath, racist jury letting go people when they were evidently guilty by all counts, disproportionate power of Governors, like petty tyrants of small, sometimes failed, States.'

'But this is politics, America is much more than that and I hold on to my vision of America the beautiful.'

13

Jeff wanted to share some of his papers with her and see what she thought. Her feedback was, in fact, very useful. It made him see angles he hadn't thought of. She too showed some of her work and was pleased to get inputs she found thoughtful.

In the Freshman and Sophomore years there were some group assignments. Jeff was assigned to the same group as Catherine a number of times and he made the most of it. A couple of times they worked together late into the night at Jeff's place, even after there had been attrition of other group members. Rajiv tossed and turned, could not sleep. The Pat Boone song 'Oh that Johnny, that no good Johnny ... trying to steal my loving baby away' from his childhood came to his head unexpectedly and got pushed away as unworthy, not in consonance with his sense of who he was.

The flirtation was subtle, natural. It could not be objected to. He wanted to get a good grade for the assignment. Catherine was hard working. She fell in naturally. She too had the same objective. Rajiv sensed some of this but he felt he could not object to it without appearing foolish. Moreover, part of him felt that he should not be insecure.

He responded by making very passionate love. He kissed her hard. Their kiss became very deep. As the kissing got really out of hand and they got totally lost in it, neither of them knew what was happening. Their total focus stayed with what they were doing. There was sweat above his upper lip and on his forehead and down their backs, the cold wind outside blowing over from the West, notwithstanding.

The wind rustled in the trees outside. *Un homme et une femme.* Their unity continued even after they both came. It was their starting point and concluding point. With her the journey was always the destination.

14

Catherine and Rajiv came to a cold and snowy New York. Rajiv's parents found friends in New York and they were happy to give him their daughter's bedroom as she was away over the break.

Initially, Rajiv worried about staying over late at Catherine's but saw that her liberal New York parents were at ease. Their daughter would fly away soon enough and visits would be so precious.

Soon after, along with Catherine's family, they saw images on TV of Earthrise through Apollo 8. This was the time of Carl Sagan and his ideas about the Cosmos.

Central Park was a fairy tale of snow and some ice. Snowflakes twirled in the air and tree branches were laden with snow; the squirrels were much bigger than any Rajiv had seen in Delhi; the people seemed so gay, dressed in colourful winter wear and even more colourful scarves. Adding to the colour were the Blue Jays, Robins and Woodpeckers hopping about. Rajiv was charmed but above all, had eyes only for Catherine. He pulled at some snow hanging like hair from a tree. 'Rapunzel, Rapunzel let down your hair,' he said. Catherine giggled and as it came off easily in his hand, fled, as she saw the intention in his eye of putting it down her back. She allowed herself to be caught and wrapped her long violet scarf around him. They kissed. Thank God, this was America and they could, flashed through Rajiv's mind, as he floated into ecstasy.

An enterprising young man was renting out toboggans. On

an impulse, Rajiv took one and pushed Catherine down a slope as she shouted 'wheee'.

At one end of Central Park, they espied the Metropolitan Museum of Art. Tempted, they went in. They could get a bite to eat as well. Neither of them wanted to wander through it in any sequential order. Too much like work. They held hands and lingered before paintings. It was like a slow dance; she was happy to let Rajiv lead.

'I have a friend who does portraits of people,' Catherine said suddenly. By what stream of consciousness, only she knew. They were in the section comprising the Impressionists. 'She has asked to do one of me. It'll be part of an exhibition by up-and-coming artists.'

A breakfast meeting was set up for the next day, the notion a bit strange to Ashok, but already quite common in America.

Rajiv and Louisa hit it off almost instantly.

Nude, Louisa decided at the end of the breakfast. She had created an atelier, in a space her father owned in SoHo. A rendezvous was set up for that afternoon.

Rajiv thought of his stomach. It was well hidden under his clothes but it wasn't flat. He stripped self-consciously. Catherine smiled encouragingly. Louisa paid no attention. She wasn't there to judge.

The place was well heated and Rajiv sat looking out at the skyline. Soon it would start putting on the lights. The time for the next session was set. Rajiv and Catherine were just here for two weeks.

Louisa was a quick worker and the painting began to take shape pretty quickly. A few more seances and she would actually be finished.

Catherine had stopped coming to every séance. She had her own things to do in her home town and she certainly didn't want to be a chaperone. She was glad that she had been instrumental in this happening.

Rajiv didn't want to look at the work in progress. What if it was unflattering? What had made him agree?

When it was almost over Rajiv felt comfortable enough to take a peek. 'I know you don't interfere with an artist's work,' he said, 'but my penis is too big and dark red. It's as if I was turned on.'

'Maybe you were. It's my perception. I wasn't particularly thinking about it.'

'Why attract attention to it? It's incidental to this being a nude.'

'That is debatable,' she said, with the hint of a smile. She looked most fetching. He let it go at that. She wasn't going to change her mind.

The painting of Rajiv would be the final work to be part of the collection to be exhibited soon.

15

'Why is photography Art?' Catherine suddenly asked.

'Because it tries to capture a moment of time and sometimes does it beautifully. Each photographer artist sees something unique and manages to communicate that,' he answered.

In the afternoon they would chat for hours and topics would easily come. When there were silences they were comfortable or the silences would be broken by some of the beautiful music that was exploding and was a speciality of the time. It was music to take you far away in your head. Her friends who were also in New York or from there would join them. Some of them smoked and that would produce a convivial haze that would enhance the music and the perception of everything. 'Cigarettes and magazines' a la Simon and Garfunkel.

'Let's go see a film this evening,' said Catherine one afternoon.

'OK, which one?'

'How about *Blow Up* of *Michelangelo Antonioni*? Another example of photography as art.'

'Lovely film, I've seen it but don't mind seeing it again.'

'It's at 5.15 p.m. It's 3.45. Plenty of time. We'll go. Relax. I'll make some coffee.'

'How many close friends would you say you have, Catherine?'

'Ooh. Let's see, there was Robin from School. I used to love it when she came for sleepovers or I went. We used to laugh such a lot together, mostly about boys and their stupidity.

Sometimes the conversation would be more serious, more heart to heart. She lives in New York and we are still good friends. She knows all about you. But these days you are taking up all my time.

'Then there are Amy and Sandra from School. They are very involved with their boyfriends but we are still close. Its satisfying talking to them and hanging out with them. In college, I have made a couple of friends but they are not from New York, so we hang out in term time.'

'Oh, my goodness. It's after 5, we'll miss the beginning. We lost track of time chatting. Let's run.'

'Should we jump into a cab, will that be faster, or the subway?'

16

Her mother, Karen, was a home maker and what a home she had made. Always a pleasure to come back to. Their home was on the Upper East side—with all that it connoted, aesthetic, sophisticated, aristocratic,warm- a refuge from the world when needed, full of books and music, paintings that captured your attention, sofas that you felt like sinking in, colourful cushions and lights that brightened the greyest day. Her father, David, was a senior Banker working on Wall Street but unlike many of his colleagues, he did not stay late at the office nor did he go for seven course martini lunches at well-known establishments from time to time. The one exception he made was when the family came to visit him in his office. It was their holiday but not his. He took them to a restaurant shaped like a chimney and bearing that name, situated on the ground floor. Family time was very important to him, as was the vibrant culture scene in New York. One couldn't be late for that in the evening. This created an upper middle-class home that did not have internal tensions and a secure environment—so important for self-confidence and dealing with the outside world. The piano at home was played by her father and Kimberley, so that their home was filled with beautiful music. The art had been carefully selected and painstakingly accumulated over the years. The bookshelves were made to measure for the spaces that presented themselves. There were many books at home that Catherine wanted to read and hadn't yet found the time for. So much to read and so little time for it, she already felt.

Her sister Kimberley and brother Brian were good looking in a different way. Initially, she felt that she didn't get the same amount of attention from her parents but discovered, over time, that her siblings felt the same. She talked to Rajiv about it. It led to her thinking of herself as lesser than them in ways that kept changing as she sought to come to terms with it. It had made her suspect rejection when none was intended in interactions, which are complex enough as it is.

Her siblings had come four years later and were two years apart. At that early age that already set her apart. There were the two of them and there was her.

The cold weather made Catherine even more beautiful. She was blossoming into a stunner. She really caught the eye. How had guys kept away from her during the summer? There must have been so many attractive young men over the summer in New York. Some of them she could have fallen for. How had she resisted advances which must have taken place? Had she?

He himself had gone to parties, talked to and danced with girls but that was it. New York and America would be far ahead of Delhi in the interaction between young men and women. If anything had happened, nothing showed in Catherine's face, except delight at being reunited with someone who had been so much in her thoughts. Rajiv looked deep into her eyes and was lost in them.

Christopher phoned a couple of times and wanted to see Catherine. She told him that she and her boyfriend had come together to New York. She was polite but firm. Rajiv couldn't help being relieved that the Christopher danger had been warded off, at least on this visit back home.

Rajiv came over early and they stepped out into the fresh morning air for breakfast. They found a cheerful family-run place not far from Catherine's. It was a German bakery. There was a whole variety of German breads, including rye. Those in themselves could have filled them up. They allowed themselves to be tempted by a typical hot sausage with mustard.

There were always unexplored, interesting places in New York. They wandered around footloose and fancy- free. They went into shops. They bought some clothes, spent time in a shop selling all kinds of clocks, another one selling Japanese woodblock paintings. They meandered around in no particular order, loving the freedom of that and letting the atmosphere soak in. 'The best way to experience Manhattan is on foot,' she said. 'Of course, subway when one is in a hurry.'

It was one of those beautiful, very cold, 'On a clear day you can see forever' kind of days. There was a talk by a well-known professor of Particle Physics from Cornell later that afternoon, on subatomic particles. Quarks had been discovered just a few years ago. It dealt with the inter-relationship between sub-atomic particles and apparently unrelated movements inter se, which actually did affect each other. It opened up whole vistas for them.

There was a piano performance the next evening. It had pieces by Mozart, Chopin and Schumann. It was a virtuoso performance and they stepped out into the New York evening with their spirits soaring. It had been a full day.

Catherine took whatever time off she could from her family and was happy to tramp around all over with him. Catherine had a number of interesting friends in New York. Rajiv met some of them when Catherine wanted to spend time with her family or had family engagements. They were wonderfully stimulating to talk to. She had been away the whole term and her family felt that she had come to spend time with them.

'She was his girl but who is whose anyway?'

'You can't hold on to anything. You can just make the most of it, as it goes by,' said Irene, her friend, as if catching his thought as they walked around in the Village, peeping into boutiques and stopping for coffee.

'Not even people?' Rajiv said.

'Least of all people,' she answered.

'Even friendships don't always last or they are not the same. People change.'

Another afternoon he wandered around West Village and Chelsea with a different set of Catherine's friends, once again unconstrained by schedule, however brief this freedom.

Catherine took him to a jazz concert in Brooklyn. Afterwards, she was meeting a group of school friends who had managed to get together with great difficulty. 'No boys allowed,' she said, giving him the briefest of kisses.

The subway involved too many changes, so a cab was voted for. He dropped her at the corner and saw her walk off into the night towards a brightly lit block of flats nestling amongst tall trees in the enchanting night light, highlighted by the surrounding darkness.

The two weeks were dream-like and in a sense a continuation of the summer weeks that had been so life changing for them in India. Berkeley was now their work base. It's not as if there wasn't the inevitable skirmish even in this short a time. But the passion in the making up more than made up for it.

On one such New York afternoon, as soon as they entered her room, they couldn't wait for the door to be shut properly. They kissed standing near the door. The bag dropped from her hands.

Rajiv bent her backwards, forcing her mouth open even more. It was a kiss as wide as that in the famous *Life* photograph where a sailor grabs a lady in New York after victory and the end of World War II had been announced, and bends her down in a deep kiss.

They straightened up and started kissing insatiably. It was like making love through the mouth. The sensuousness of it filled them up. This wasn't going to stop here. Their total focus was on their union above and below. They put everything into it and forgot the world. But they went slow on the ecstasy, lest the fragile magic of the moment slip out of their hands. It had the explosive potential to build up very quickly, with the depth of feeling involved.

It was their starting point and concluding point. Travelling in the Himachal mountains with a stream flowing across the road. A vast green valley on either side, with majestic, mystical, mysterious blue snow topped mountains at the end.

They varied the tempo but it built up. He pulled out. 'Funny that the same pubococcygeus muscle should help one to stop peeing and to control ejaculation,' he thought fleetingly. The effect was titillation, though his motive had been self-control. He couldn't stop now, she felt. He started again. She was already high. Things built up on top of that. Rajiv felt a fountain of youth wanting to burst forth within him. They reached a crescendo of unity. It was over the rainbow. It felt like it to both of them. They lay next to each other sweating, exhausted.

They kissed mouth to mouth again. Then gradually the kissing became deeper and much more intense. There was that familiar throb to it—the metronome—one of the trademarks of their long afternoon kisses. And then he was inside her again. His penis became very big and penetrated way, way inside. She felt it was so deep it reached her navel. She also felt it filled her up completely. And then there were lights in the sky, music in the air, waves on the beach, gently lapping the shore.

They had made so much of Delhi, New York had incomparably more to offer. There was something happening all the time, everywhere. On top of that this was the late '60s, with its inventiveness in music, writing, films and plays.

Just before they returned to the West Coast, a vernissage of her latest oeuvres was put up at a well-known gallery. The social glitterati of New York were there, he gleaned from the media present. He hoped it would get good reviews.

Louisa greeted him with a kiss on the mouth. After all, she had seen him nude a number of times. Did she linger a second longer? Maybe it was to make up for not acting on his comment on the painting.

This was yet another unique American custom, which didn't seem to exist anywhere else. Good friends, maybe very good friends, when meeting or parting would kiss on the mouth, in hello and goodbye. It was intimate yet social. It was an interesting in between category, to convey the continuum, the rainbow of emotions and feelings. It was a part of the accepted culture; it was the counterpart of the French social kiss on both cheeks or the Belgian kiss on three sides. It was clearly social, not quite sexual, not erotic. It was always between men and women. It was brief and always closed mouth on closed mouth. Yet it was at least a shade, a degree more intimate. It was on the mouth.

17

Back in Berkeley, Catherine would sit in the library for hours, fully absorbed. Rajiv, when studying in the same Library, would get distracted by her presence, her aura. After 45 minutes of concentrating, he would want to take a mini break and go and sit next to her, scribble her notes. But she would have none of it. She would shoo him away or her answers would be very brief and clearly discouraging of an interchange. She didn't even want him sitting on the same table to study, although each bench had six study spots on either side.

In this term there were parallel and overlapping courses in Elizabethan and Renaissance English Literature and just Shakespeare. There was also Jacobean Literature with Shakespeare straddling both Elizabethan and Jacobean. Catherine could choose any one or two out of the four. Choice also depended on which Professor was considered the most engaging and lucid. Also, on what Mark and Jeff might choose, (though this thought was unacknowledged) and they, in turn, by her choice.

She was veering more and more towards choosing English Literature as her major, anyway. They all had equal credit. That helped. There were three different outstanding Professors teaching these four courses. It would be interesting to see their takes. She started off with Elizabethan and Renaissance but with Elizabethan alone, Catherine would miss out on detailed focus on plays such as *Othello*, *King Lear* and above all, *Macbeth*. She decided to switch within the time limit from Elizabethan to just Shakespeare alone in his different moods under two different sovereigns. This was especially possible as the Professor for Elizabethan Literature and Shakespeare was the same. Before she left the course, she heard the Professor extol literature written during the reign of Elizabeth, in the latter half of the Sixteenth Century as a splendid period. The Professor clarified that there was no discernible common denominator, however, of the writing of the time, and it merely referred to the period.

She ended up choosing the broadest and the narrowest of the four—Renaissance and Shakespeare. Shakespeare because she enjoyed his writing so much and Renaissance (1550–1660, more or less, she told Rajiv) because it would cover that whole period when England was trying to catch up with Continental Renaissance, which had started much earlier, that too in Florence, Italy, not even France.

'Outrageous!' said Rajiv, grinning, getting a light slap on his cheek in return. 'It wasn't confined to Literature alone,' she continued, 'but was a broader cultural and artistic movement.'

'I know this,' Rajiv interjected.

'On the Continent, it didn't just start with Art and Architecture; the European Renaissance revived interest in ancient Greek and Latin literary and philosophical texts. Copernicus, a true Renaissance polymath with his knowledge of astronomy, mathematics and other subjects, proposed the theory that the Earth revolved around the Sun and not the other way around.'

'Yes, and there was Galileo, who used the telescope to look at the heavens, and amongst his many discoveries, he supported Copernicus' theory that planets revolved around the Sun and not the Earth,' Rajiv filled in.

'This was heresy to the Church, which believed then that planets circled round the Earth. Galileo's love of Geometry helped his work. He was able to make out the Milky Way Galaxy as individual stars. Galileo published his work as a mathematical proposition but did not save him from being pilloried. He was forced to recant under threat of Inquisition and placed under house arrest for the last years of his life,' Catherine continued.

'The Renaissance had man at the Centre. The Mediaeval ages in Europe had God and religion at the centre. Renaissance Humanism turned away from that and put man's creativity, freedom, progress at its core. It looked for inspiration to the ancient Greeks and Romans. There were other ancient civilisations but that's all the Europeans were aware of,' said Rajiv.

Catherine ignored that tangential thought and continued, 'Renaissance covers a vast period but unlike Elizabethan, its common theme is the multidisciplinary attempt *a rattraper* to catch up with the rest of the Continent, including in Arts and Philosophy,' Catherine continued, ignoring him. 'Renaissance would cover Elizabethan anyway, just in less depth.'

'Characteristics of Renaissance poetry were wit, beauty, and truth,' she said, savouring the idea. 'Poets used repetition to emphasise their themes.'

Rajiv was privy to these decisions and gave her his opinion. A couple of times, Rajiv came and sat in, in her classes. He could, though he couldn't raise his hand and ask questions.

John Donne too straddled the reigns of Elizabeth I and James I and his metaphysical poetry was covered in the Renaissance. Rajiv, with his philosophical upbringing at home, was a great help when Catherine discussed some of the intellectual complexity.

Giving an overview of the times, the Professor said Poetry flowered, including new forms like the sonnet and blank verse. This was a golden age of drama as well. Thomas Dekker wrote *The Shoemaker's Holiday* and other plays, Christopher Marlowe, his well-known *Dr Faustus*, Ben Jonson with his acid satire *The Alchemist* and others, considered by some to be next only to Shakespeare as a dramatist.

'Some of them were polyglots, like Lyly—writer, poet and playwright, who wrote, amongst other things, *Euphues: The Anatomy of Wit*. His literary style was known as "euphuism", we learnt in class today.'

'Oh, is that where euphemism comes from?'

'We'll have to check the etymology,' she said. 'Don't know. Could be.'

'In English, did novels develop earlier or was it the Theatre or Poetry?' she asked, quizzing Rajiv soon after class another day.

'The novel, I imagine,' said Rajiv, 'followed by Drama and Poetry.'

'Wrong,' said Catherine. 'Poetry, followed by Drama and then the novel.'

'Hmm, who would have thought, given the relative output and sales today of Prose, Drama and Poetry.'

'You have a point—especially the prominent displays of fiction at the bookstore nowadays and the coverage in the news media but it wasn't so.'

'Another thing that was noteworthy, Rajiv, was the role of the sovereign in its influence on Literature at the time. Spenser, one of the most important poets of this period, composed *The Faerie Queene* in celebration of Elizabeth and the Tudor dynasty.

'Why, even periods in English Literature have the appellation of the ruling deity. *And playwrights adapted and played to the liking of the monarch.'

'They must have needed patronage.'

'Precisely,' said Catherine. 'They needed to make a living.'

'Was it only from the Monarch?'

'There was patronage from other aristocrats, too. Plays were performed in Courts. And there was a Censor for Plays. To make sure nothing was said against the monarchy. So, authors used historical plays when they wanted to say something even obliquely critical. It had to be clever, indirect.'

'Plays were only in the Courts?'

'No, there was the Globe and seven other theatres, for the hoi polloi. The Globe burnt down and theatres were shut down during outbreaks of the Plague. Parliament shut down all public Theatres in the 1640s and only two reopened subsequently with the Restoration.'

'When did Elizabeth pass on?' asked Rajiv.

'1603 or 1604,' came the reply.

'And Shakespeare?'

'1616.'

'What about Poetry?'

'Poetry was for private circulation. The printing press was becoming more important during the Renaissance. And typesetting was highly labour intensive.'

'I'm learning a lot, Cath, and you make it so interesting. Maybe you'll become a teacher, eventually.'

'Prose had writers like Thomas More with his idea of *Utopia* and Philip Sidney (who was more a poet) with his *Arcadia* and stories within stories.'

'Like the Mahabharat,' said Rajiv.

When she mentioned Thomas Hobbes, Rajiv said, 'Oh, that's my subject, I probably know more about that. I've read *Leviathan* but please ask your professor whether he thinks Rousseau is better known for his *Social Contract*.'

'It would not be until the next century before *Gulliver's Travels*, *Robinson Crusoe* and *Moll Flanders*,' Catherine told him, narrating what the Prof. said when she raised her hand and asked about Jonathan Swift and Daniel Defoe.

18

Undergrad in America was clearly not like post grad from what Rajiv saw and heard. Across the spectrum, from the more serious to the less. It was a fun and party time, a time to experiment, explore and find yourself and your interests, amongst other things. Students coupled off. Many of those relationships broke off, some sustained. Studies were not the main focus, were almost incidental to being there.

Given those premises, Catherine, the fun-loving free spirit, also worked hard. Rajiv had seen how intelligent she was from the time he met her. Her grades in school had reflected that. She continued to be at the top of the class in college too. Her reading, her thoughts, her conversation portrayed that.

When she was with Rajiv, she was fully there and they both had a blast—for instance, when they listened to Bach or Brahms in their rooms, leave alone at a performance. They had late evening dialectics with their friends on Raymond Aron, Simone de Beauvoir, Michel Foucault, Roland Barthes, amongst others, sometimes at protest sites.

She embodied the best of flowers in your hair late '60s America. But Rajiv wanted more of her, and that she seemed not to be able to give. He took it up with her. She laughed.

'As you get older, will this tendency get accentuated?'

'Who knows?' she laughed, looking appealing.

'That's a risk, you'll have to take, *cherie, n'est-ce pas?*'

He wanted to possess her, knowing that you can't own anybody.

'Catherine, there is a French film festival on at the Film Club. There are some lovely films on contemporary. Do let's go.'

'I would love to, Rajiv, but have you seen my reading list? There is no way I could get through that and come.'

'You are meant to select, Catherine, not read every book in the list. Nor read every chapter. C'mon, we won't get this chance again in a hurry. There is *Une balle au coeur, Jules et Jim, Vivre sa Vie, L'annee dernier a Marienbad* and many others.'

'I won't enjoy it, Rajiv. Have too much on my mind. That'll remain at the back of my mind. Go with one of your buddies or Robin. She loves films. I won't mind a bit.'

Some Friday nights, Catherine would happily go dancing with Rajiv to the discotheque, but some others she would be reluctant.

'We've worked hard the whole week, Catherine. You love dancing as much as I do. Let's go. It'll be good to get out of our minds.'

'What you're saying is absolutely true but I'm not on top of things. Besides backlog in work, I've got too many chores. Who will do them?'

'I'll help you with the chores, Cath. Also, with some of your work.'

'You're so sweet. Really. But leave it, this time. It won't work. Next week, promise.'

Those years were hormone driven and there was a lot of pressure to be with the other sex. So early in her college time, could Catherine just be with Rajiv, settle down? It wasn't only boys who sowed their wild oats. Women's Lib was in full force.

As the second term of the year progressed, Mark too started feeling that he shouldn't always be just waiting in the wings. His overtures became more insistent, more calculated. Catherine liked Mark but she began to see that he was no longer content with that. She was loathe to lose his company, the biking to Tennis, the feeling of well-being she got with him but things were heading to some sort of denouement. Rajiv sensed some of this and that created a host of feelings. Things would not remain at this point. Could he lose Catherine to competition?

They got invited to some of the fraternity parties and in turn got jealous when one of them flirted or got flirted with to an extent the other one found hard to tolerate, in the age of Love Ins. Intellectually, they tried to accept it but emotions would not be contained. They judged themselves for it by the new norms but instinct had its own life. Catherine, with her flair for dancing, executed a beautiful Tango with a fellow student, equally skilled but Tango by its very nature is Tango. Rajiv tried to look away, focus on the person he was dancing with. When she came back to him, flushed and ravishing, he wanted to make passionate love to her straightaway.

Catherine made it a point to attend, to find time for Feminist happenings, be it a demonstration or a reading and a couple of times even a seminar. Rajiv believed in the cause and though his Senior Year's requirements, as well as those of his subject, were different from those of Catherine, he tried his best to make time whenever he could. Why were the loves of his life feminists. 'Or was it a coincidence,' he thought to himself. Often, he would find that he was the lone male in attendance and this pleased him. It almost became a badge of honour. Some prominent personalities made an appearance at Berkeley and Catherine would try to engage with them afterwards, young man in tow. But he differed with Catherine, who sometimes did not acknowledge the differences. Rajiv argued that he respected women as they were and thank goodness for the differences. It was part of the attraction. But Catherine would stick to her guns.

No relationship can stay at the same even high, particularly for people who felt as deeply. 'There are bound to be highs and lows,' Rajiv found himself thinking. But could they drift apart? Or were these just his fears about something treasured. Drifting apart would be so painful, especially if one or the other sees it and is helpless to stop it. It has its own momentum.

One Friday morning he picked her up early before class for a spin; they found themselves heading nowhere in particular. The very early morning had its own beauty and there was this sense of time to spare. Soon, they found themselves on roads leading out of town. Signs started coming up for Monterey and Carmel. With an unspoken agreement they followed those directions. It was time for class.

They parked near the beach in Monterey and traipsed to it. There was information everywhere about how rich the area was in sea life. The Pacific stretched endlessly and placidly beyond the horizon. Catherine took over the wheel and they went on to Carmel. A charming, romantic village, with boutiques and art galleries. They wandered around hand in hand and forgot about lunch. Classes would be over in Berkeley. This was another world a couple of hours away. They would spend the night here. They wended their way to the beach and spent the rest of the day there. Catherine attracted looks from youths next to the ocean. They witnessed a magnificent sunset with a sky of gold, orange, red and amber. It suffused the surface of the clouds. There were tinges of violet. 'Red Sails in The Sunset' came to Rajiv's head and he sang it. Catherine joined him.

They heard a French father tell his young son, '*Regarde le ciel, comme c est beau.*'

'*Exactement,*' said Catherine and smiled at them. They waited till it sank into the sea.

They suddenly felt hungry and stopped at the first attractive looking restaurant they encountered in the village on the way back. Fortunately, it was early enough and the restaurant had one other couple. No fuss with reservations. California wine was just attracting fame and respectability in the salons of Europe, even Paris, and the first sip of chilled Chardonnay had Rajiv say 'delicious' to the waiter. What else to go with it but light, airy, nutritious sea food. They chose a platter.

Not far from it they saw a brightly lit white cottage. It said 'Hotel'. The days of Internet and prior reservation had not yet come. They asked if they could see the rooms and they chose a corner room with large windows on the first floor, (though here in America, the ground floor was called the first floor, sounding strange to Rajiv's ears).

The hostess saw him filling up the address. 'Far from home,' she said.

The room was very cosy. They could hear the sea waves in the night. 'Strawberry Fields Forever' came on the radio. Lennon sang 'Nothing is real...' Catherine said, 'Nothing is permanent in this impermanent world.'

'Yes, everything changes anyway.'

Rajiv produced some Weed from Berkeley. They smoked and chatted on a host of topics as they came up, until they drifted off to sleep.

Catherine: 'Thoughts cannot be seen but they are real. And often, they are the precursors to intention.'

Rajiv: 'They make us what we are. Thoughts are immensely significant.'

Catherine: 'Thoughts have energy. It's important to have positive thoughts.'

'Sometimes, when I read something really good, I read it again. But I wonder if I should. Do I get that much more out of it? Does it justify the extra time and the inevitable boredom?' Rajiv said at one point.

'Probably not. Life is too short anyway. And there is so much other good stuff to be read. Even if what I've just read is really profound or appealing,' she responded.

What with the intensity of everything they were doing, the spontaneous visit to this magical place, both woke up before sunrise. It had been a sweet, sweet sleep. Only a few hours but the quality of sleep had refreshed them. The early morning light as it appears at the far end of the world began to touch the sky.

They sat silently. Catherine thought of something Virginia Woolf had written. 'Having such excellent communication, they could sit on a porch without saying a word, and come away feeling that was the best conversation they ever had, or something like that,' she said.

After checking out of the hotel they drove without a destination in mind for a while. They stumbled upon signs for a 17-mile drive. The Ranger type person at the gate was most welcoming and charged a modest fee for the car to enter. They encountered a number of Redwoods. Was this the Redwood National Park?

As they were leaving the area, they saw the clouds over Carmel, Monterey. One often thinks that one will come back, one doesn't like to acknowledge that one may not. Often, one doesn't, even if one is young.

19

Back in Berkeley it was again crazy days. The Bee Gees sang 'Massachusetts'—'...Gotta do the things I wanna do...'

The sense of endless beautiful days, of possibilities that they had felt in Delhi, stayed with them, albeit in a slightly different way. This was undergrad life in America. The pressures would come later. Papers had to be submitted in some courses during the terms, called semesters in the States, and their grades would be calculated towards the final score in the course. The attempt by the administration was also to keep Berkeley students, with their long history of protest, as busy as possible with ongoing assessments in different formats which counted towards their final score. The professors had the power to assign different weightages to term papers, presentations, final exams, etc.

Leisure was the biggest aphrodisiac, leading to frequent, intense, rich and varied love making. It happened automatically, instinctively. She wrote in her journal and hinted at how satisfying it was when she wrote to her best friends back East.

They would listen to 'A Hazy Shade of Winter' or 'No Salt on her Tail' or 'The Sound of Silence' as they drove out from Berkeley without a destination in mind, in the vast California countryside, with the sky and the landscape mirroring what was being sung about and the feeling that this is it that they had got when they first started going out every day would continue. 'California Dreaming'.

Rajiv liked barfi and mithai. Catherine not only enjoyed desserts but had a flair for making some of them.

'I've made Apple Pie for you today,' once when he came home after class. He could see the pleasure and the pride. It was very good but she gave him a large helping. She saw him struggling with it after a while.

'You didn't like it,' she said, in a becoming, mock hurt manner.

'Of course, I do,' hastening to finish it.

Rajiv always enjoyed the very process of opening a wine bottle. Though it might be a matter of time before corks gave way more and more to new age tops, outside Europe. 'We'll relish the cork pulling out ritual for the moment, Raj,' Catherine said, as he lowered the arms of the wine opener and drew up the cork. He smelt the aroma of the red wine. It was wonderful. It was already at room temperature. He poured them a red wine glass each. They intertwined their arms and said *sante* simultaneously. The tensions of the day, including any inter se ones, began to slip away.

Another afternoon after a particularly intensive day in classes, Catherine wanted to get out of Berkeley. She got behind the wheel and drove them to a charming place in San Francisco she had heard about. It had atmosphere. Fortunately, the tariff was affordable. A street away, the houses had typical bay windows.

They had an aperitif, soup and some salad. That was enough. They would go home and open a bottle of wine. They walked up and down the streets with some of the lights already coming on. The evening wind was acquiring an edge ... Rajiv put a companionable arm around her.

Back home, Catherine put on Dvorak—'The New World Symphony'.

'Most appropriate,' Rajiv smiled, before closing his eyes. The music was thrilling. They heard things in random order. It was as close as you could get to shuffling vis a vis classical music, and heard Brahms, Haydn, Schubert, Tchaikovsky, Rimsky-Korsakov...

She put on Strauss and Rajiv put an arm around her waist and waltzed her around the room. They cleared some more space in the room for a dance floor. He held himself ramrod straight and was pleased that had not forgotten how to Waltz, from the time of the parties in High School.

'You dance well,' she said, as he twirled her in the waltz and she did a little pirouette. Catherine's love of sport showed in her agility and ease on the dance floor as well.

'Oh, I thought you were going to say divinely!'

Before further banter could take place there was a faux pas and they were down in a heap on the floor, laughing.

'You were saying ...' she said, always a tease, after they caught their breath. She was right on top of him. He kissed her from below. She returned the kiss. They lay there exhausted. Didn't have the energy to get up.

Rajiv woke up late, late in the night. What had woken him up? It was 3.45 a.m. Catherine turned around; her fair body was visible through her light blue, light as a feather nightie.

It was a clear night. A sliver of the moon shone brightly. He caught a glimpse through the window. He lay for a few moments, looking at it. He didn't make any attempt to sleep. A night wind breezed in through the window, left slightly ajar. 'Constant change. Life is constant change,' he thought. Just float with it. Never try to hold on to it. You can't.

The next day there was a performance of *La Traviata*. Catherine had managed to get tickets through her network.

'Hurry up. We'll be late.' Rajiv dressed quickly and rushed in the cool blue evening to the opera. He always took longer than her to get ready, she teased him, 'I'm the girl.'

It was a very good performance. As good as the others they

had individually seen. They knew the story well.

'Ah, Verdi's music,' Rajiv said, almost to himself.

'What?' she asked, turning up her face innocently. Her upturned face was too inviting to be resisted. He kissed her.

They walked laughing at some of the crazy things Catherine described getting up to in High School, through sloping streets, indistinguishable from the many students around. Catherine jumped on his back with her legs sticking in front and said 'giddup'.

'Stop horsing around,' he said, whilst galloping.

Back at Catherine's they kicked off their shoes and lay down on the sofa. They were cramped on it. He pulled her down on to the thick rug below. He kept his underwear on but she laughed and pulled it off.

'Wait,' she said, shivering and pulled down the blanket. They lay in the same position. It enabled maximum contact.

'Wait,' it was his turn to say.

'Not if I can help it,' she added mischievously. She started doing things designed to blow his brains out.

20

They kept exploring each other emotionally and sexually and traversed new frontiers every day. The possibilities were endless. The journey of discovery with one person, if it is a person one has fallen in love with, can have infinite variety. They added to their repertoire other aspects of foreplay and lovemaking.

One day, they reversed positions and she lay on top of him. He met her other mouth. He kissed her there. And then she was actually kissing him there –had taken it in her mouth. She flicked her tongue around its tip. He became huge but she seemed to manage. It was the first time. She kept switching between his mouth and penis and it was hard to say which was more pleasurable. Nothing else mattered then. Knowing that he loved her added such depth to it.

She sat across him on the table, not even wrapped in a blanket, and they talked for a while. He liked looking at her. She didn't seem to mind the cold now.

As the semester progressed, they came across two couples, Ron and Jean and a bit after that, Billy and Nancy, who had become good friends of theirs and who had seemed inseparable, breaking up. They had been together from High School in Berkeley. They were both shocked. It seemed so improbable.

'Nobody from the outside really knows what happens between two people, except the two people themselves. And sometimes they don't understand fully themselves,' said Catherine.

'When it's one sided, one partner doesn't want it—not only

is that partner heartbroken but also sometimes mystified,' she continued.

'Do you think it gradually built up between Ron and Jean, Cath, or it was sudden? Breaking up suddenly could be to do with jealousy or infidelity.'

'Though jealousy could grow too,' she said.

'And disenchantment could be to do with habits becoming too much for the other, gradually,' put forth Rajiv.

'Something in the other person starts to irritate you— and this grows. And then sustained irritation breeds counter irritation. Or sometimes, very little things. Below the surface,' elaborated Catherine.

'What about Billy and Nancy?'

Catherine shrugged. 'It could also be that you love someone and then you feel that something inside you has died ....'

'... that inexplicably, you don't feel like that anymore, for reasons you can't explain or even understand yourself,' Rajiv completed the thought.

'Do you think it happens more with one gender than another? More to do with emotions? It's more complex than caprice, though it could be as inexplicable.'

'Probably deeper too,' Rajiv added.

'I don't think so. It could happen either way. In the case of habits that annoy, it can increase or the other one accepts them, more or less and gradually learns to live with them. It ceases to matter as much,' Catherine said.

Rajiv continued the chain of thought—'Marriage or living together is a lot to do with expectations. If the gap is too high between expectation and perceived reality, it can be hard to bridge. If it is more realistic or not built up too much, it doesn't create a hiatus.'

'Often, when the other becomes the one, expectations

increase—that leads to more problems. So long as you are boyfriend/girlfriend, especially living apart, the expectations are less and the gap is not too high,' Catherine agreed.

'But sometimes, problems don't emerge even after people start living together. Somehow, only after marriage,' said Rajiv.

'How do we know this? We are young and idealistic…' started Rajiv.

'… but observe the world around us,' completed Catherine.

'Could this happen to us? Is there an incipient danger? Or our relationship start to get jaded?'

'Of course,' she said smiling and kissed him, and the storm clouds that had gathered an instant ago, got blown away by the wind.

21

One evening in the Berkeley Hills, as they looked down at the glittering City, as Rajiv looked pensive, Catherine asked him what he was thinking about.

'About the system for electing the all-powerful US President, actually. He is not elected by a majority of the American people. The majority may even lie with the losing candidate. The voting system is a complicated system for a society that likes and values simplicity, where corporate leaders teach 'Keep It Simple Stupid' (KISS). The Electoral College system misrepresents the intention of the people. It gives an amplification to even a slight majority.'

'How do you mean?'

'In most states, all the Electoral College votes for that State go to the one winning, even if by a few thousand votes, thus distorting the scope of victory. The winner might have won by a small margin but will get all the votes of that state. What kind of tomfoolery is that?

'It's the other extreme from proportional representation but I'm not even thinking of that. The first past the post Parliamentary majority system, like in Britain, has its shortcomings but this is worse. Elections are at the heart of democracy. Consider Party primaries. Some of the selection of party nominees in different States is at Primaries, some at caucuses. The systems for electing party candidates are not transparent, nor clear cut—it can be by show of hands, head count, etc.

'They vary greatly from State to State and between the two major parties in each State. There isn't even voting in some of the

Caucuses. US Election laws do not apply to Caucuses, Primaries, Conventions. Then there are Primaries that are closed—only for Registered Party members (though when they can register also varies), Semi closed—unaffiliated voters can also participate, open primaries any voter can vote, semi open primaries.

'The idea was to take away power from the party leadership but then party bosses themselves are often not elected and have come to their positions through a series of operations. The idea may have been a good one but in practice this is disputed, especially by academics. De facto, party bosses exercise a great deal of power... By presenting only certain candidates at the state and city level, one is influencing the choice.'

They sat companionably for a while. There were just the sounds of the night and the somewhat distant sound of the Bay Area below.

'America is the most powerful nation on earth. Yet, the defence budget is really high and rising, both in absolute numbers and as a proportion of the GDP. The Pentagon wields enormous power and influence. So do various lobbies. America was built on the railroad, just as recently as the 19th century but the automobile industry lobby has virtually closed down train travel,' said Rajiv.

'Yes,' added Catherine. 'There is the gun lobby, the right to bear arms, the only major nation which has so many people carrying arms.'

'*The* evangelical lobby, with its very substantial inflow of funds, with such a different puritanical and proselytising brand of Christianity from the one in Europe,' continued Rajiv.

'The pharmaceutical lobby—sometimes adverse effects turn up later but millions of dollars have already been invested by big Cos,' took up Catherine.

'And then there is the power of money in elections. It

should have no role but has a ginormous one.'

'Yes, I'm aware of that, Rajiv. If that affects choice—whither democracy after that. I wonder why Academics and intellectuals don't take up these issues more strongly.'

'I've really wondered about that myself. Up till now certainly not enough and often when they do its within certain confines. They don't go beyond that. This may be changing now in the Sixties. If ever there was hope, it is now.'

'Oh yes. And there are exceptions, like Noam Chomsky.'

'Either the rest are playing it safe or there is a certain political consensus. Or they justify it by invoking the wisdom of the Founding Fathers. Or they hide behind statistics and jargon and their analyses don't cross a certain unspoken line. Plus, there is a very strong built-in inertia against substantial change in the system. They would have to push a Sisyphean rock against gravity. They would have to use the system to alter it and how tough is that,' Rajiv added after a pause.

The next morning, he woke up to see Catherine still asleep; she looked so beautiful. Leonard Cohen's '…like a sleepy golden storm' came into his head. He gazed at her for a while. Then bent down to kiss her. She kissed him back as she awoke and sat up against the headstand. She had that morning look in her eyes, still not invaded by thoughts, innocent, appealing.

22

Student life was changing everywhere. There were straws in the wind that it would introduce co-ed dorms in early 1969 with 24-hour visiting hours. Stanford and Michigan were even more liberal about this. Marijuana was freely in use.

As *Life* magazine put it [22], boys and girls could see each other as people. Sometimes, boys and girls spent the night in the same room without sleeping with each other. Lot of platonic relationships developed. Boys and girls stopped being objects. This led to an ease and naturalness of behaviour. Could go for advice when they were down or depressed even if they happened to be from the other sex. Some of them came from homes where overt emotional display, including of love, was not encouraged. Loving was not experienced as much as needed, leading to loneliness. Students got more emotional room and support to address questions like 'who am I' and to relate to others more openly and expressively. There was sex but not more on account of co-ed living. The fears of some parents were not realised. It didn't lead to promiscuity. Students made the rules themselves and that worked much better. There wasn't resentment or rebelliousness against imposition. The idea, very daring by the norms of even the early '60s, leave alone the '50s, became widespread in many campuses because of the pervasive impact of the powerful cultural and sexual revolution of the late '60s. Academic standards did not falter, may actually have improved because of being able to study together.

In Europe this openness went even further in the late s60s.

In Communist countries like Poland, where religion was actively discouraged, all the more so.

The attitudes to boy-girl relationships were swinging 180 degrees as depicted in movies as recent as in the '50s, where sex before marriage was inconceivable, to intercourse attached to being in love rather than to being married.

In the Bay Area amongst others, it went further at the time in what were clearly revolutionary changes. Rajiv and Catherine discovered that there was actually Free Love amongst some young people. It was considered not being tied down. Both were open minded about not passing judgement on those that subscribed to this. No one imagined at the time that AIDS would change everything in the '80s. What they did like was that girls could ask guys out. Or say 'I like you,' to someone.

Rajiv would go over to Catherine's dorm or she would come to international students' house. They spent most of their time in one place or the other. International House was economical, very comfortable and well located. The same applied to Catherine's dorm. But neither of them knew if they would last the year living separately. The following academic year they would definitely start living together.

There was subsidised University housing. International families lived there, but others too. Lots of non-students hung out there for the fabled Berkeley experience.

There were no mixed dorms as yet but everyone could sense that it was round the corner. In any case, girls and boys could go in and out at all times. Couple of dorms were on Durant and some in Bancroft Ave Houses. In any case, undergrad dorms were all near campus. There was fixed rental housing around the University, fixed rental places on College Ave. Single Grads too were in dorms. Married student housing was considered in Campus, as were next door dorms.

Living together also started becoming fashionable, not just for those who were in love and did not believe in marriage as an institution or were not yet ready for it, but for convenience. Marriage was not so important, especially in the Undergrad years. In the Grad years some of the girls wanted to marry. Sex and love were separated. A boy and a girl could live together to save money and for companionship.

Would Catherine and Rajiv wait till the next Academic year to live together? They wanted to live together now. They were both very well ensconced. There were practical considerations.

If they gave up their separate residences, where would they find good accommodation in the second half of the academic year, unless someone was leaving just then? Highly unlikely. They tried all the same but after a month of looking, had to give up. They would plan for it in the Fall Semester. She would still be an Undergrad but he would go on to his next degree.

23

Rajiv came over to her dorm nearby, with every intention of going back but the love making kept him there and neither of them was satisfied with once. When he woke up next to her, he found her giggling. 'Look in the mirror,' she said, by way of explanation. 'Devil,' she added. Two locks of his hair at either end were curled up in opposite directions.

Rajiv always knew that he wanted someone passionate. Catherine matched him, passion for passion. They shared passionate kisses, had late night conversations, and the eyes, the expression of one would light up when thinking or talking about the other.

'Dreaming, I'm always dreaming' by the Cascades played on the radio. Catherine saw Rajiv looking at her. She laughed.

'Are you looking at me significantly, Mr Jones?'

'Well, aren't you? With your head far away in the clouds …'

Even if they had quarrelled, she would smile and he would be charmed. Or an accidental brush of her shoulder or contact with her hand. Nothing else would matter.

California had its own wine and some very good ones as Rajiv and Catherine were to discover to their pleasurable surprise. He poured some red wine from Napa Valley and rolled it around on his tongue, savouring it.

Rajiv picked up a book from the book-shelf and read aloud. It turned out to be Camus. He read out an extract—it was about *cinq minutes de puissance*, a petit functionary exercising his power to harass people. She slapped his hand away from the book, stuck her tongue out mischievously and put on music. She got up and started Boogie-Woogie-ing. Who can read when there is dancing? She put on *Stoned Soul Picnic*. Catherine shuffled the music and they switched the dance to match it—Jimi Hendrix, Small Faces, The Cream, New Faces, Nat King Cole, Chuck Berry, The Kinks, Herman's Hermits, Buddy Holly, Lindisfarne, Laura Nyro—some '50s, but stuck mainly to the '60s.

'Look at us,' said Catherine, with self-awareness. 'Classic examples of the times—'60s music, Existentialism, grass, emancipated thinking.'

'Where is the grass in this?' said Rajiv.

'I thought you'd never ask,' eyes betraying the barest hint of mischief. 'Voila! I have one hand roll with no tobacco in it.'

Rajiv took a drag and passed it to her, letting everything soak in, as the music continued.

A movie hall around Shattuck had a screening at night of *A bout de souffle*, something they had both wanted to see and hadn't had the time for. Nothing was far in Berkeley. They peeped into another show, *Darling*, with Julie Christie. They would allow themselves binge watching. The film was very good but they felt sleepy and left it mid-way.

In one of the neighbouring parts of Oakland that looked and felt just like Berkeley, Catherine met Rajiv for a coffee just after class. The young man behind the counter saw a pretty, radiant girl and picked up on that.

'What would you like today, a double latte?'

'And sir?' he enquired, looking at Rajiv.

Rajiv's eyes fell on one of the books she was carrying. 'I see you are reading Heidegger these days,' he asked her. 'How come?'

'This is an excellent translation of *Being and Time*. It completely changes it.'

'Yes,' Rajiv nodded. 'Translations are so important and a

good translation involves so much skill and creativity. They deserve a lot more credit than they get. But Heidegger?'

'You'd be surprised. One may not agree with him but being liberal means being open. And he wrote a lot more than the Nazis selectively took. He was an environmentalist.'

Another time they were in the Poets Corner quarter of Berkeley.

Catherine said, 'You know, thinking about political parties, there are only two parties in our country, whereas reality is a myriad shades. In everything. It's too binary. It's only slightly better than a one-party system.'

'Yes, political preferences go along a Left to Right spectrum, with opinions on some issues that queer the pitch and cannot be strait jacketed. But even leaving aside that complexity, two is over simplified. It's too Cartesian. It reduces to this or that.'

'It becomes a charade, a mockery of choice,' Catherine supplemented. 'How many brands of shampoos or toothpastes are there for the American public to choose from? There are over 300 types of roses …'

'… and more than 1500 types of mangoes in India alone. The human complexion is a continuum of tones and hues. An ultimate distortion is to call it black or white.'

Rajiv continued the dialectic, 'There are nascent attempts but the one thing in which the two ruling parties join hands— sometimes not even in passing the budget of the American government—is in keeping down third parties, leave alone Independent candidates or anything remotely like the Social Democrats in Europe.'

'It's easy to be branded communist in America, which is a no no. Almost anti-national,' Catherine said.

'Ballot access laws make it difficult to even come before the voter in a ballot.'

Back at Rajiv's, they put on some music. 'Don't let me down'. 'Ooh—just love it,' said Catherine.

'Don't let me down, Don't let me down,' they sang along. 'I'm in love for the first time, Don't you know it's gonna last.'

Then, 'My Sentimental Friend' by Herman's Hermits and 'Nashville Skyline'.

As winter moved to spring and it was the month of May, People's Park happened. The University of California's parking lot was converted to a park by students. It was more a symbolic protest rather than the thing itself, as Rajiv observed to Catherine. A group of drummers entertained people. Governor Reagan called the National Guardsmen. They also surrounded anti-war protestors; an unarmed spectator was killed. Rajiv and Catherine found themselves in the thick of it. Nausea gas was used on a peaceful rally in the rose garden.

There was a long student strike in nearby San Francisco State University. Catherine found time to go one day and participated. But she also treated herself to a long browse at the City Lights bookstore and came back with two books she would relish.

Many times, Americans had disagreed with wars they felt were unwarranted but the big difference was conscription. That made the opposition to it much more personal and immediate. The Bay Area was among those that remained at the forefront of it.

Meantime, The Who came out with their Rock Opera *Tommy*, The Archies with 'Sugar Sugar' and Crosby, Still, Nash & Young, who had started the previous year in California, rose in the charts. On the celluloid front *Midnight Cowboy* came out, followed by John Wayne's *True Grit*.

'*Hair* has just come out to super reviews. Let's see if we can get tickets for it, Raj,' Catherine announced.

'Oh yes, I've heard of it. There are lovely musical and theatre productions like that being put up. Do let's go.'

'It is one of counterculture's many significant contributions to creativity and human understanding, as per the media.'

Catherine and Rajiv became habituated to many regular Berkeley happenings. One of them was the Friday noon rock concert that featured many of the creative bands that the late '60s were producing so many of. Some of them were better known only in the Bay Area but their music was foot tapping, lovely to listen to. They would play at Lower Sproul Plaza, which was central and not far from the main campus entrance at Sather Gate, through which and in front of which so many student demonstrations took place. Demonstrations also took place at Sproul Plaza, more inside the campus and next to Sproul Hall, the seat of the University Admin.

The University, with its more than 300 feet bell and clock Sather Tower, one of the tallest in the world, standing symbolically, dominated the ethos of the town, all the more with its bells and carillon concerts and the associations with the music department. They got used to seeing the clock tower and the archway over the main entrance every day.

Lower Sproul Plaza was right in front of Zellerbach Hall, where all the formal campus musical performances took place. Catherine and Rajiv looked forward to both the lively rock scene mid-day Friday, the sounds of which floated all over the campus, and the evening classical music performance where they joined the formally dressed crowd flowing into the Plaza in the break.

There were also the Wednesday noon concerts of classical music. They were often in the open air, with the musicians setting up stands and tuning their instruments. The sound would waft all over the University. It had a different feel to the ones in the auditorium.

The University had some impressive ceremonies, including

the commencement ceremony at the California Memorial Stadium next to International House, no less impressive than those of the most storied Universities back East.

Rajiv and Catherine enjoyed the many parks in Berkeley, including Tilden, one of the biggest. They came across many couples hanging out in them. The young people weren't all students. Some of them couldn't go home because they were still living with their parents. There was Lake Anza, Jewel Lake, unique trails. They created *inoubliable* memories for both of them.

Undergrad life was larks, they discovered. For Rajiv it was a happy continuation of the three years that had ended all too soon in College in Delhi University. For Catherine it would continue for some time. For Rajiv next year would be grad life. He hoped he could fulfil Grad life requirements and still have a blast.

They browsed in and picked up gems at Codys books on Telegraph, as free thinking a place as Berkeley itself, opposed to any form of censorship.

Some days Rajiv and Catherine browsed in the shops on College Ave and in front of Campus. They went into some music shops and bought some albums.

Catherine enjoyed looking at bric-a-brac and at Antiques. Sometimes, her keen eye would come across a find. Rajiv wasn't very interested. 'Not cultured enough,' he told a smiling Catherine. But he still liked being with her. Sometimes he did her Photostats in this time.

At other times he carried some of her heavy cyclostyled material that the professors gave out. The first time he did that it was raining but there were no puddles in street corners. 'Sir Galahad,' she still said, as if on cue.

University of California was a very unusual State University and could hold its own with the best private ones. They became aware that Berkeley was the jewel in the crown and the biggest public university of seven campuses. It managed to attract and home grow a prestigious faculty.

Berkeley seeped into their cells along with its avant gardism and free thinking. Berkeley also did corporate research for major corporations. So far so good. But it also had a nuclear weapons class for Govt. This was not so comfortable. The students were fighting to abolish all nuclear weapons. The admin started opposing the bringing up of non-Campus issues, whereas the thinking of the students was, by definition, universal. Intellectual enlightenment knows no boundaries.

University got over around 4 Some days the classes they had chosen got over earlier. The number of undergrad classes per week varied. More courses meant more credit but Professors cautioned students about getting too ambitious and taking on too many courses. The research papers alone that were required per course would prove to be quite a handful and they would all count towards the final score. Meantime, they accumulated the necessary units; many of the courses they took gave them four units instead of three. They studied next to each other for the mid-term semester exams. He would find out about the grading system in grad school.

He had made some friends with Grad students. There were some aspects that he already liked. Classes were called. Profs. invited students to their houses often for Grad seminars and started the discussion. The atmosphere was stimulating, convivial. There wasn't fear about how things sounded, what others might think. Research papers had to be given in, in seminars. Those had to be of high quality. For Graduate work there were three seminars a week. A Grad class had eight people or so. A class was about 1 ½—2 hours. There would be about

100 pages to read.

It was a continuation of the supportive ethos of the undergrad lectures where the numbers were much higher. Attendance was taken in undergrad but it wasn't serious. Class participation mattered for much at both levels.

Unlike American kids, Rajiv had not grown up knowing how to repair day to day things. It was cheap to get repairs done in the shops in India. In America it cost a lot, so one fixed it oneself. Rajiv wished he could handle these things the way everyone else did. Some of the gas stations required jamming the hose with a lot of force into the tank and holding it that way, otherwise the meter would stop. Rajiv had difficulty with that. Catherine was supportive from the start, though such things made him feel inadequate.

Jeff started rising to the forefront of the student movement; he had ideas and was a good speaker. He started coming across as charismatic and was poised. The top student leadership was mostly composed of more senior students but he was amongst those that came into the notice of Sproul Hall. His grades were good, his professors liked him, he didn't give any opening for picking on him. The Professors were quite different from the Administration. Many thought more or less like the students.

Jeff had other plans. If at the end of the academic year Rajiv went to India for the long summer break and Catherine didn't accompany him, Jeff could try and replace him as her beau. He was falling for her and all was fair. It was also clear that there were boundaries and there was a certain point beyond which she wouldn't go.

Catherine was increasingly attracted to him, in spite of herself. She liked all the attention she got from guys. She liked hanging out with them. She didn't have doubts about how she felt for Rajiv. But she really was so young, they both were.

It led to their first fight about another guy. It started with something else. But it quickly came down to this. Things below the surface came up. It escalated.

'I don't believe it. You're surely not jealous?'

'Of course not but we could have done things in that time together…'

'We are not always free at the same time…'

'You could have caught up on your work so you'd have been free later on…'

'We can't be so calculated, Rajiv. What happens to spontaneity?' she cut in, her voice rising.

'Besides, we need to interact with other people. We expect that of each other.'

'Of course…'

There was a knock on the door. A Swedish neighbour wanted to borrow some sugar.

'The other day, after the dance for your year, when I came to pick you up, you were sitting so close on adjoining chairs.' Rajiv felt his heart beating fast as he said this. He knew he was embarrassed. He felt like sinking into the ground. He wished he hadn't taken this up but it had been said now.

'Am I hearing right? Is this you talking?' There was a sharpness to her voice. He felt a twinge of pain.

Both were aware that the exchange was becoming heated. It might spin out of control. All sorts of things were coming out. Many of them not intended.

Catherine stormed out of Rajiv's room. She came across a friend on the street and tried to talk to her about an upcoming demonstration but couldn't and left abruptly. She lay down on her pillow and cried. Rajiv put his face in his hands.

Rajiv had the sense of a calamitous thing happening. He had wanted things perfect, there was nothing more important.

He had fought with someone he cared intensely about, was so in love with. Was this the price of being young and idealistic—is this what it meant? He loved her so. That too about a guy. It was so demeaning.

Catherine's feelings mirrored Rajiv's. Ridiculous. But they had quarrelled. They had quarrelled before, like couples do. Sometimes it was about little things. Minor friction points would unexpectedly surface and at times it escalated. She would contradict herself.

'But earlier you had said this, Cath,' but she would just get irritated.

Catherine was sensitive and perceptive, if anything. That had been evident from their Delhi days. Their relationship wasn't based only on common interests or common values; the differences added to the richness and the interest.

He would go over in his mind what had caused the tiff and let it go after a little while. She too would *laisse tomber*, not seek a resolution. It was always worth it for both. They knew these were not significant, bound to come up, as relationships became longer. When they laughed together it was still like always. And sometimes, one thing would lead to another and they would laugh interminably.

They didn't see each other for three days this time, despite the longing for each other and the intense sense of loss that both feared if they did break up. Those three days seemed like a lifetime. They also knew that this kind of blow up was inevitable between a couples. But meantime it didn't take away from the end of the world nature of it.

He came across her on University Ave. Their eyes met and looked into each other's and knew that the row was over.

There were exams at the end of each year in undergrad life but both Catherine and Rajiv were good at them, knew how to max them, and buckled down to study for them when the time came. There were students who studied consistently and perhaps that was the better system but temperamentally neither of them did it that way.

Rajiv's Grade Point Average thus far was a perfect 4 and Catherine's was 3.6, the highest being 4. She told Rajiv that she would catch up in the years to come. She had a long way to go.

What would Rajiv choose for his Masters—Political Science, International Relations or Math. Rajiv, for practical reasons, decided to stick to Math for his Masters. It would give him the manoeuvrability to add a number of subjects if he so wanted or go into further specialisations. There were new developments taking place. A new field called Computer Science had come up in 1968. It was a part of the Department of Electrical Engineering. If it kept its promise, it could become an independent Department in time. In High School most of his subjects had already been in the Sciences. In the Bachelor's he had chosen a Physics minor.

'Rajiv, I've more or less decided I'll choose English for a major. I enjoy Literature very much and it opens up so many windows into so many worlds,' Catherine said dreamily.

'It'll be lovely Cath, though what will you do with it afterwards? Have you thought of that?'

'One step at a time, *mon cher*,' she said smiling and all he could think of was the smile.

A magical year was coming to an end. It had gone like a dream. Rajiv's only undergrad year. Catherine would still have more.

Catherine decided she would come to India for half of the long summer vacations. After that they would start to live together. No couple was perfect, they both knew, and there were bound to be adjustments. They had already started looking. Places got snapped up quickly and everybody planned ahead in America. She would spend six weeks at home in New York with family. She hadn't seen them a long time and she missed New York.

Catherine came as far as she could at the airport and kissed him. A kiss that would linger on both their lips for hours afterwards. It was a 'Leaving on a Jet Plane' [23] moment. Again.

> 'There's so many times I've let you down
> So many times I've played around
> I tell you now, they don't mean a thing…'

Before their lips met, they found themselves looking into each other's eyes. Rajiv and Catherine knew in that instant more than ever, that they did want to get married. The passage of time after the engagement only confirmed this. Whatever might have been or might be the ups and downs of a relationship over time.

She watched the plane take off, till it became a blur, a distant hum.

On the long journey home, he lay in a reverie. 'I had Catherine. And was I grateful to the Cosmos for that! I better believe my great good luck in having her.'

24

Rajiv missed Catherine a lot during the six weeks without her. But he understood well that she needed time in her home town with her family. He too was glad to be in Delhi, in his house with his parents, to sleep late, to have everything done for him, to be free of deadlines. And the biggest miracle was that she would join him half way through. They wouldn't be without each other for the whole three months.

Some of the people he had come across in Delhi University flashed through his mind. They had all dispersed. Some of them had been such characters. Some of the young women had seemed so unattainable. 'Maybe when we remember other people and places, like the ones we studied at, it's partly our own growing up that we remember, how we were,' he thought.

'And Ayesha—what of her?' Thoughts of her unexpectedly come. Much of their courtship had been in Delhi. When he passed those places, he was reminded of her, of her laughter, the way she flirted (which was so different from that of Catherine) and how pleasant she was. But Ayesha had long left these wind-swept streets with the sun shining on the pale brown bark of the tall, stately trees and disappeared into the horizon.

Momentous things were happening. Man walked on the Moon in July 1969. It was unbelievable, the stuff of Fantasy. The whole World saw the images, was united and rejoiced.

John Lennon and Yoko sang 'Give Peace a Chance'.

Easy Rider came out with Peter Fonda. Jack Nicholson said, 'This used to be a helluva good country. I don't understand what is going on with it'.

Woodstock took place in the middle of August with about half a million attending. For three days, so many well-known groups got together, the rain and the mud and the impromptu lodgings notwithstanding. The atmosphere remained one of peace and love. The overriding thing was incredible music, fun and harmony. It was the flower children at their best. The Lovin' Spoonful saw the number of 'Beautiful People', the atmosphere and said what many felt—how unbelievable it was. Rajiv was sorry to miss it but was also happy to be home.

Catherine would join him in Delhi for the second six weeks. They hadn't been sure that she would be able to do that. Half the American summer vacation would be over. August was so hot in America and it would be the romance and beauty of the Monsoons in Delhi.

'You'll have to manage without me,' she said smiling and then rewarding him with a kiss.

A lot can happen in six weeks or 'a short bit of time' as Catherine and Rajiv had discovered the first time they had met, all the more for people as intense as them. Some young couples they knew had broken up because one or the other hadn't been willing to wait for three summer months when so much happened between boys and girls. Sometimes it coincided with one of them suddenly becoming aware that it was the end of an era—a beautiful one but I have to go, keep moving.

25

Rajiv loved his family, his parents, his city. How would he abandon everything, make a life elsewhere? What would Catherine do in India? Too active and too creative a mind to be not employed in worthwhile activity. The answer was clear to both of them. They had to be together. They had to find ways and means to overcome the practical obstacles. Life was only worth living with the other.

The six-week separation when she went back to New York increased the longing. She missed him and felt she should be in Delhi or Berkeley with him, the comfort of home and the city she had grown up in, notwithstanding.

Time would decide where they lived and what they did. For the moment, she had to complete her course. Either she would eventually come back to India with him. After finishing her education trajectory in the States, maybe some work experience. She had loved India on her first visit. The second visit, round the corner, would confirm that impression. Rajiv had seen that foreigners either loved India or hated it, so unique was its feel. She would create or find her vocation there. Or Rajiv would become an entrepreneur in the land of opportunity and follow the American Dream. At the most, an even longer parting may be in store at some stage, but the power of true love would see them through.

He told his parents that this wouldn't be a long-distance relationship of any length. They were serious *malgre* their youth. They would eventually live at one place. There was a good chance it might be India. In any case, he would visit as often as possible and so could they. They would not lose him.

Rajiv survived the separation. At long last, the six weeks got over. He waited at Delhi airport for the familiar face to emerge.

The guest section of Rajiv's house was comfortable and spacious. It had a large bedroom with en suite bathroom and a sitting room. It was connected to the main house through a long verandah. It couldn't have suited Rajiv more. It gave the comfort of the main house and the independence and privacy of a separate unit. Rajiv carried her suitcase up the four steps to the verandah. Catherine walked in to flowers in every room.

Catherine quickly settled down. She got turned on by the romance of India. She wanted to see some very romantic Hindi movies. He took her to a replay of *Chaudhavin ka Chand* and when they stepped out, the sky was appropriately filled with a bright moon playing hide and seek behind the monsoon clouds. He took her to *An Evening in Paris*. She laughed at the unintended caricature. As the *Indian Express*[24] later said 'the unbounded hedonism of Hindi films of the '60s had a devil may care attitude appropriate to the Swinging '60s. They had colour, optimism, flamboyance'.

She adored Shakespeare Wallah, Ruth Prawer Jhabvala's writing—the history, the ruins, the charm of the interactions. Mughal Delhi, with its spectacular orange, red and violet sunsets on Lodhi Road.

They went to concerts in the evening, which carried on late into the night, of Panna Lal Ghosh and Chaurasia with their haunting evocative flutes, not just the famous sitar of Ravi Shankar but many talented sitarists like Vilayat Khan, Pandit Nikhil Bannerjee, and others like Imrat Khan that were coming up, Amjad Ali Khan with his sarod, the tabla of Zakir Hussain, the veena and the santoor from Kashmir. Star filled nights which captured the romance of India, the night jasmine—*raat ki rani* being sold outside the classical music setting. He wore starched white kurta-pyjamas, she looked ever so fetching in colourful, graceful sarees. The music lovers would be sprinkled around on the thick double mattresses covered with crisp sparkling white sheets, reclining on bolsters or sitting comfortably cross- legged. There was a starting time but one could come in anytime and find a place. It would end when the artistes got tired or the audience grew too sleepy or sparse.

There was a host of monuments scattered at random all over Mehrauli. Some of them were Mughal, most of them were pre-Mughal. Pillars and remains of several old temples are also lay scattered in the park. [25]

Unlisted, many of them in danger, in urgent need of repair, being saved from encroachment. That also gave it an organic wildness that created its own charm. There were over a hundred monuments, including a Rajput fort from 1060 AD and architectural relics of the subsequent period of Turkic, Afghan rulers—Khilji, Lodhi dynasty, etc.

She went shopping for textiles, jewellery, handicrafts, miniatures. Her suitcase would be overloaded.

She came across exquisite fabrics, silk, pashmina, Cashmere, handcrafted work, kalamkari, papier-mâché, items made from walnut wood, nutcrackers. Some items, like those made from Teak, were too heavy to take but she could surely export some of these to New York and California. This could be an avocation. There was so much potential. With her parents' network, it could be big.

The six weeks in Delhi were those of heightened and spontaneous fun. It re-ignited what they had experienced last summer, the charm of the courtship, the special feeling of those first moonlit nights in Delhi. There was only Rajiv for her.

Rajiv took her to the calm of the Rajputana rifles temple in the Cantonment area; she felt a peace descend on her. They went at dawn one day to the Purana Quila, where only the early morning freshness accompanied them. Catherine told him later that at times, she felt that she was visiting the place centuries ago, that the present was the past.

The Cellar was still rocking; they got lost in the dancing and the music, amongst the convivial crowds, till late in the night. India continued to remain a magnet for the late '60s generation. Lots of young foreigners continued to pour in, to find themselves. This was the heyday of the late '60s—its epitome. Everyone was here in India. All the beautiful people—'How does it feel to be, One of the …'

The Sensations at Maidens was different. Here too, they forgot everything in the dancing. They went in circles, bending up and down like Red Indians and letting out war cries. The psychedelic lights were something else. Wheels in Ambassador Hotel provided more variety. They would come back soaked with sweat.

They went for drives in the Monsoons—the darkness would seem unreal and all enveloping. Some very early mornings took them to the ruins at Lodhi gardens, though here they always found a few others, no matter how early it was; the only other place matching that would be the nearby Delhi Golf Club. They went to Buddha Jayanti Park—the paths leading nowhere, especially as the clouds became tenebrous and there was the imminent threat of rain.

They explored Chandni Chowk and the bye- lanes of Old Delhi; seven cities had existed here, the Tibetan market on Janpath and the treasure trove of book shops further down, Cottage Industries and the finds there, the eating there impromptu at Bankura, the many boutiques coming up everywhere, with lovely Indian clothes of a variety of fabrics, psychedelic designs. They ran out of money at Blow Up, the new boutique at 1 Bhagwan Dass Road.

She developed a taste for seekh kabab, shashlick, Chaat and stood outside the shop in Bengali market and had gol gappas filled with chick peas, potatoes and maroon tamarind water or green mint water. She enjoyed the light dosas and idlis in South Indian food restaurants, the rich variety of vegetarian food in Gujarati restaurants and Marwari homes, the fish preparations with coconut from Kerala, the Chicken Tikka in Moti Mahal. She enjoyed the drama and adventure of going at 3 a.m. to the Coffee Shop at The Oberoi.

Rajiv took Catherine to a restaging of *Tughlaq* at the National School of Drama. It was the heyday of Alkazi. It was about a Turkish origin ruler of India, who decided to shift his capital from Delhi to South India to be safer from the threat of Mongol invasions in the 14th century. India, because of its manifest affluence, had been under constant threat of invasions not just from Muslim nations to the West but from the North as well. They went to a staging of Pirandello's *Six Characters in Search of an Author* at AIFACS's atmospheric auditorium, next to the British Council. It regularly staged plays. Catherine said it was delightful. He took her to performances at Little Theatre Group, with its consistently good repertoire. Soon after the break-up of India, it had put up Chekhov's *Three Sisters* in Hindi. [26]

Through the open window looking out on the front garden, they saw a very blue afternoon sky above them, with gossamer cottonwool clouds. There were huge ones and smaller ones on the background of a pastel blue sky. Everything was sleeping—the squirrels and parrots in the garden, made drowsy by the golden afternoon rays of the sun; a breeze blew in from outside and fanned his face joined to hers. She loved the colour of his olive chest. The fan breeze felt pleasant and cool on his sweat.

The second visit, albeit only six weeks, felt no less emotion filled, intense, than the first one. It was six weeks only if one counted in days.

26

Rod Laver won the US Open, making it two Grand Slams. Both Rajiv and Catherine admired his way of playing hugely. Other Aussies, Roy Emerson, Neale Fraser loomed largely on the scene. Touch master Ramanathan Krishnan had made it to the Wimbledon semi-finals twice a few years earlier. Manuel Santana was the other player who played tennis like chess.

Butch Cassidy and The Sundance Kid was released to much acclaim.

The Beatles came out with *Abbey Road*. Their fans had wondered if they could maintain the high creative level they had reached with 'Sgt. Pepper's'. *Abbey Road* had beautiful music, which remained in one's head.

One of the Beatles was shown on the cover, bare footed. Rumours went around in a few circles that something had happened to him. Fortunately, they didn't last. Few were to guess that it would be the last studio album the band would record together. But music lovers would feel, in the time to come, that the sum of the parts had been infinitely greater.

It was around 10 p.m. Rajiv went into the guest wing. *Abbey Road* was being shuffled on the radio. 'Golden Slumbers' was playing. She was getting ready to sleep. 'Come Together' came on, followed by 'I want you so bad' followed by 'Oh Darling, Please believe me, I will never do you no wrong…' Catherine looked at him with such intensity. They kissed. As it escalated, some of her clothes came off. Rajiv got up and locked the shining brass chitkani. A half clothed or scantily clad person is often far more exciting than a naked one. There is the promise of further treasures, conquest.

She bought such fancy exciting slips and panties of different colours and some of them were such brief briefs that it made for maximum visual appeal and contact with her skin. She sat astride him in bright yellow briefs, her legs and thighs brushing against his. She pulled off her pantie, whipped off his underwear and sat down on him, coming down diagonally on him. He became absolutely enormous inside her. She moved up and down, sometimes going so far up that he almost came out of her. She rode him like a stable horse.

'Ride 'em, Cowboy,' he said. She laughed and kissed him. He arched his back to get the most out of their kiss. Their mouths were open very wide now and were joined like two halves of a circle. They pulled at each other's mouths just the right amount to maximise pleasure and to maintain the kiss. It was very important to keep kissing while lovemaking. It was a dual connection, which added immeasurably to the quality of lovemaking, to the quality of unity. They kissed and fucked and kissed and fucked. There was nothing beyond this in life.

27

The long journey to San Francisco required a change of flight and a stopover in Europe. Rajiv would stop a couple of nights in an *Auberge de la jeunesse*. It made the journey much more bearable and the transition smoother. It also helped with the cultural transition. The old world still had its own warp and woof, its threads of commonality, some more evident, more on the surface, some less so. Europe and India had those obvious differences that made the West the West and the East the East. But they also had much in common which was at a subtler and profounder level. It was no coincidence that the Indo-European languages were part of the same group.

It was not just a stepping stone, maybe the differences between America and Europe were as great as those between Europe and India, albeit in disparate ways. On the surface there was the common European origin of both, but America had evolved in such a unique way, as uniquely different from parents as offspring can be. And that was without even taking into account the intensive mixing of diverse European cultures within America and the effect that produced.

A Polish student on the next bed in the dorm talked about vodka. It is made from potatoes and one of the healthiest hard drinks. It is odourless and colourless—often very useful in many situations! The most significant difference is that you gulp it down. If you drink it fast, it doesn't go to your head; if you sip it, it does. So, you tilt your head backwards and knock it down in one go. Polish cavalry officers, as an expression of their macho-ness, would stand at the very edge on the window ledge of the brightly lit chandeliered room, with the snow glistening way below in the darkness of the night. They would drain the vodka glass in one gulp, tilting their head way backwards and smash the glass against the fireplace. Those who dared did it again with their subsequent vodka glasses, still managing to keep their balance. In front of Westerners who didn't know, one could always show off and gulp down glasses of vodka without getting high, since it was the best way to drink it.

Catherine was there at the airport to meet him. It is always so nice to be met, no matter how many times one travels. She looked svelte and fetching.

The next afternoon, she suddenly pulled him out and sat astride him with her back to him; she took hold of it and guided it in as she sat on it; facing the bay window in San Francisco. The sensations were quite different. And its suddenness was exciting. There were a lot of firsts.

A friend had invited them to hear some music and check out her music system, which she was selling as she was getting a fancier one as a present from her parents. She'd gone out for an errand in between.

28

New students were pouring in. Fresh new faces shining with the same idealism. Catherine was a Sophomore, still more in the lighter undergrad party time of the second year, though The faculty tried to give them enough workload to keep them busy and to maintain the standard of excellence.

The Admin had a different motive, to keep them as occupied as possible, to leave as little time as possible for them to protest or to think about deeper questions of values, of how things should be in the University, in life and in the larger outside world—the sort of idealism that created dissatisfaction and wanting and believing that a better world was possible.

Rajiv was in Graduate School. It was another ball game now. The pressures and the requirements had altered. Rajiv had a different kind of workload and the rhythm was different. They moved into Graduate Housing together. They had applied well in time, as per plan.

They got up earlier just so that they could have breakfast together before rushing off for class. In Rajiv's case, the group session started even earlier than Catherine's first class. In the late afternoon they tried to co-ordinate their schedules as far as possible for a workout together, be it just a run together. They invariably felt much better after that.

They were more at home in Berkeley now; America and the West Coast no longer felt like a strange New World. They went to movies, shared impressions of new books they had read, new music that was pouring out from all over America.

Catherine talked about intelligence as different from empathy; Rajiv added sensitivity to that—how some of the greatest minds did not have the latter. Not just scientists, inventors but even creative people in the arts. How you would expect them, at least, to have sensitivity and yet, oddly enough, it wasn't there—especially in personal behaviour or the most important relationships with their family. Several well-known examples came to mind.

29

'Let's get married, Rajiv. I love you so.'
       'I do too. Let's.'

Reunited in the Campus life of Berkeley and living together, Catherine and Rajiv decided that it was time they got married; they were older, they were ready now to move beyond being engaged. They had been together long enough and now it was more painful to be not united in marriage.

They would have a church wedding followed by a Hindu wedding. They chose a date in October.

New England that Catherine went often to with her parents for the Fall foliage and which she described to Rajiv, showed him photographs, would be in full bloom. Fantabulous. It would have been another World had she decided to study there. Was there a fleeting moment of regret? Not really. She would not then have been a co-student with Rajiv, nor a denizen of Haight Ashbury.

Her parents and the rest of the East Coast aristocracy would fly down. A ball was planned before the wedding. They would not be satisfied with just the normal wedding festivities. They would want another special event.

Rajiv and Catherine compiled their guest lists. They would try and keep it to people they really wanted but both were people's persons. Catherine had a last-minute request. A Pakistani girl has just joined the University. She is such a nice girl. Could she please bring her along? Catherine couldn't say no to Karen, she was her best friend in Berkeley. She would talk to her only as one can to a girlfriend, when she had words with Rajiv, for example. Karen's parents had asked her to look after this girl. They had been at the UN mission in Kashmir, which straddled both sides of the border.

Rajiv wore a dark maroon velvet suit. Catherine looked ravishing in her flowing white dress. Her mother had suggested something from Fifth Avenue but Catherine chose her own dress in San Francisco. Karen was one of the bridesmaids.

Catherine made quite an entrance to the Ball on the arm of her tall and stately father, in an apt dress rehearsal for the Church wedding entrance, as the orchestra struck up 'I could have danced all night'.

Sitting on a corner seat was the Pakistani friend. She had just known that Karen had invited her to a typical American wedding. The names hadn't been relevant. Everything was a blur. She was still getting her bearings in this strange and distant land. Ayesha had really flowered and become even more captivating.

Acknowledgements

Niranjan Koirala for valuable inputs on Berkeley

Himanshu Koirala for detailed inputs on Berkeley

Ameeta Rathore for many suggestions and comments on first draft

Manju Kapur Dalmia for suggesting shift to Berkeley

Manish Purohit and Kavita Bhalla for editorial help

Vasudha Dalmia for suggesting Berkeley, dvd *Berkeley in the 60s* and inputs on Mount Holyoke

Girish Rathore for help with research on Berkeley, especially maps of the time

My family—Manju, Maya, Katyayani, Agastya for all round support

Karine Schomer for input on the Berkeley semester system

References

1. 'Satisfaction' a song sung & recorded by Rolling Stones
2. 'Ticket to Ride' a song sung & recorded by The Beatles
3. Raza, M. Hanif, *Portrait of Pakistan*, Ferozesons Pvt Ltd, Lahore, 1994.
4. Whitehead, Andrew, *The Lives of Freda: The Political, Spiritual and Personal Journeys of Freda Bedi*.
5. Ibid., p. 170.
6. Bourke-White, Margaret, Halfway to Freedom, Asia Publishing House, Bombay, 1950, p. 172; Whitehead, Andrew, *The Lives of Freda: The Political, Spiritual and Personal Journeys of Freda Bedi*, Speaking Tiger Books, 2019, p. 258.
7. Wheeler, Richard S., *Politics of Pakistan—A Constitutional Quest*, Cornell University Press, 1970.
8. Rushdie, Salman, 'Pepperpots', *Midnight's Children*, Jonathan Cape, 1981, p. 291.
9. 'Strangers in the Night' a song sung & recorded by Frank Sinatra
10. 'These Boots are made for Walkin''a song sung & recorded by Nancy Sinatra
11. 'Sounds of Silence' a song sung & recorded by Simon and Garfunkel
12. 'Black is Black' a song sung & recorded by Los Bravos
13. 'Monday, Monday' a song sung & recorded by The mamas & the papas
14. 'Summer in the City' a song sung & recorded by The Lovin' Spoonful.
15. https://www.wellesley.edu/ accessed on 29 November 2022.

16. Kitchell, Mark, *Berkeley in the 60s,* Susan Griffin, Mark Kitchell, Stephen Most (writers), Mark Kitchell (producer), 1990.

17. Judt, Tony, *The Memory Chalet*, Vintage Books, London, 2011.

18. Judt, Tony, *The Memory Chalet*, Vintage Books, London, 2011.

19. Kitchell, Mark, *Berkeley in the 60s,* Susan Griffin, Mark Kitchell, Stephen Most (writers), Mark Kitchell (producer), 1990.

20. https://en.wikipedia.org/wiki/Allen_Ginsberg#cite_note-95 accessed on 29 November 2022.

21. Ibid.

22. 'Co-Ed dorms on Campus—An intimate revolution', *Life*, December 7, 1970 issue.

23. 'Leaving on a Jet Plane' is a song written and recorded by singer-songwriter John Denver.

24. https://indianexpress.com/article/entertainment/bollywood/1960s-bollywood-classic-films-mughal-e-azam-guide-4913491/ accessed on 29 November 2022.

25. https://en.wikipedia.org/wiki/Mehrauli_Archaeological_Park#cite_note-5 accessed on 29 November 2022.

26. https://www.ltgdelhi.org/history accessed on 29 November 2022.

Printed in Great Britain
by Amazon